RULED BY

by

SARA RAWLINGS

CHIMERA

Ruled by the Rod first published in 2000 by
Chimera Publishing Ltd
PO Box 152
Waterlooville
Hants
PO8 9FS

Printed and bound in Great Britain by
Omnia Books Limited
Glasgow

RULED BY THE ROD

Sara Rawlings

This novel is fiction – in real life practice safe sex

I could feel my nipples rubbing on the coarse fabric that papa ordained for our bodices, for they had become inexplicably hard and sensitive. I believe it was fear that caused this habitual condition just prior to punishment, and despised myself for my cowardice. I resolved to show exemplary fortitude tonight, to make amends.

But despite my resolution, my hand still trembled as I knocked on that forbidding panel of oak.

A New Beginning

I remember that Marion felt it should be she that went up to papa after supper.

'After all,' she said, 'I am the eldest, and responsible for keeping house. It is not as though papa's complaint is of some specific fault, the onus for which we could decide between the three of us, but a declaration that an example should be made to ensure a devout attention to our duties in future.'

'But Marion,' exclaimed Charlotte; the middle sister at twenty-four, three years younger than Marion and four years older than myself, and very tender towards us both, 'your buttocks were well thrashed only two days past. I dare say you are still sore in your drawers, he beat you so.'

'Charlotte, I blush to hear you speak thus,' Marion replied. 'In any case, we do not customarily display the results of our corrections, and you would not have been aware of the state of mine, if you had not slipped into my room when my mind was on other things.'

'That I can well imagine,' Charlotte said, 'since you were lying across your bed with your skirts up, and your drawers down to cool your burning bottom. I only came in because papa had spent so long over you, and Annabel and I were worried for you.'

'I know, and I am grateful for your concern. Papa's rod is sometimes hard to bear.'

'All the more reason why one of us should go up this evening,' I put in. 'Your bottom is not yet recovered enough to receive it again.'

'I shall come to no harm,' Marion replied. 'Has not papa assured us many times that providence, which made woman the weaker vessel and prone to give shelter to all manner of evil, also endowed her with the wherewithal to receive correction in full measure without risking injury to health? I will steel myself to do my duty, and attend papa's study at seven, as he requires.'

She paused momentarily. 'I would make one request of you though, my dear sisters. Perhaps you would be so good as to see that the supper things are properly cleared away, and the house secured for the night. I doubt not that, after my interview with papa, I would prefer to remain in my room, and seek to learn how best to profit from the lesson he will have taught me.'

After supper, which we took alone, papa preferring to have his brought to him on a tray, where he was preparing his sermon or other uplifting text, Marion kissed us both warmly, then gathered her skirts to ascend the stairs to papa's room, moving a little stiffly, for her bruises still troubled her.

She was a long while gone.

We heard just a trace of papa's loud rumble through the heavy oak door. He seemed to have considerable matter to impart. Then there came the faint *snick* we all dreaded so much. We remained in the kitchen, so did not catch them all, but it seemed a fearful count. Towards the end we heard several sharp cries accompanying the snicks, then Marion screamed, her cry answered by a bark from papa.

The rhythm of the correction paused, them resumed. Another few beats and Marion screamed again. Our hearts stood still, our bellies quaked. Marion was very brave, but papa seemed to have penetrated her defences.

In the silence that followed we waited to hear her leave the dreadful chamber, but the door stayed shut. After a few minutes we could hear, dimly but distinct through the heavy wood, a regular thump, punctuated by groans from our dear sister.

Finally all was quiet.

Several minutes later we heard the door open and shut, and Marion's footsteps, dislocated as if she was limping or walking with stiff and parted legs, dragged across the landing to her room. We looked at each other but did not voice our unspoken thoughts. She had asked to be allowed to recover herself in private, meditating on her correction, and we would respect her wishes, and turned to clear the room and secure the house for the night, as we had promised her.

Marion did not, however, keep her room that night. You may imagine our astonishment when, a bare half-hour later, the door opened, and there was Marion, clinging to the frame. She shuffled across to us with an awkward gait, then, instead of joining us at the table, where we sat, dropped to her knees at the end of it, her bowed head on her arms. We jumped up and ran to her side, endeavouring to raise her and set her in a chair, but she resisted.

'No,' she said, her face lined with pain, 'let me be. Papa beat me most severely, and I cannot manage to sit.'

We urged her to let us assist her to her bed, but again she refused.

'Before he beat me, papa lectured me on the shortcomings of the household, and what he deemed should be done for the improvement of our souls, through the mortification of our bodies. He specifically desired me to acquaint you with the gist of his argument, though the details will have to await another occasion as, not only did he spend some time giving me examples of our shortcomings and what means we should adopt to correct them, but he made it quite clear that these were but by way of example, and that he would be expanding and expounding his thesis continuously.'

My heart sank and my knees trembled at this dire news. Our father had brought us up to fear God, and more particularly, God's surrogate on earth, himself as head of the family.

I should perhaps explain at this point that, though we called him papa, and treated him in all respects as if he had indeed been our progenitor, this was by way of a courtesy title, albeit one so engrained in us that we never considered it. He was not in fact a blood relative, being the husband of our late mother's childhood friend, who had accompanied our parents on their ill-fated trip to Paris and perished with them when the packet to Dover foundered in a gale. Her relict took us in, and we were cared for by his austere housekeeper, until Marion had reached an age when she could take over the duty, and relieve our benefactor of the expense.

Since our parents' death in my infancy, we had known no other source of knowledge, guidance and discipline. There were not even servants in the vicarage since Marion attained the age of sixteen years and was put in charge of the housekeeping, with Charlotte and myself undertaking more and more domestic duties as we grew older.

We had of course, daily women from the village to do the rough work in laundry and scullery, and even assist with periodical major cleaning and refurbishment, but we were expressly forbidden to engage in any but the most necessary conversation with these women, who were, in any case, too hard-driven to be communicative, and returned to their homes as soon as their allotted tasks were done.

We had, besides, a groom and a gardener, but neither lived in, and both were directly employed by papa, and we scarcely saw or spoke to either.

Our regime was already one of stern and biblical patriarchy, and if this was judged too lax and in need of additional discipline, then our failings must be lamentable, and the necessary correction vigorous and searching, and Marion's brief digest of what our stern guardian proposed for us did not fall short, nor did we expect it to, for we knew he would never shrink from his duty to curb the evil which the bible, and the church, teach us is inherent in all women and, especially it seemed, in the women of his household.

When Marion had explained the impossibility of her

sitting at table, Charlotte had run to fetch a cushion from the drawing room, and now she knelt on it as on a hassock, in the attitude of prayer, her elbows on the table but her head lifted so as to address us.

'It would seem,' she began, 'that our father is conscious of a certain undesirable element within the household, an evil effusion of the feminine. As he has so often taught us, the Holy Book, St Paul, the ancient Fathers of the Church from St. Augustine onward, are all agreed that we women are sinks of iniquity and vessels of unrighteousness. It is not enough that we try not to sin, hopeless though that task may be for our sex, but we must actively mortify our flesh and discipline our minds, so that our feminine emanations do not disturb the meditations and prayers of a man of God, such as he.

'Naturally, he intends to help us all he can by increasing the frequency and severity of the corporal corrections to which we are subject, in the hope that we might derive some benefit therefrom, as my flogging tonight was intended to demonstrate. But he feels that mere fustigation in itself will not be enough to enable us to drive down those dark forces within us, which are a snare for men, dragging them down into the pit of hell, for which we women are already irredeemably destined.'

'But what new disciplines must we be subjected to?' I cried. 'We already accept his every ordinance as befits dutiful daughters, conscious as we are of the obedience we owe our father, and all other members of the superior sex. How may we serve him further?'

'You are right, dearest Annabel,' my sister replied, 'we

do owe him absolute obedience and, I believe, we make what poor effort we can to deliver it. But we are but poor weak women, prone to stray from the strait path of virtue at every turn, and we need to reinforce our resolve by submitting ourselves to a harsh discipline to rein in our naturally wayward ways, and teach us virtue. Papa is drawing up a comprehensive list of the penances and disciplines we must impose on ourselves and, when he graciously presents it to us we will receive it with gratitude, thanking him for his care on our behalf.

'At this time,' she continued, 'he has only vouchsafed to us his first suggestion for our spiritual health. He requires that we are to give up the sinful luxury of hot water for washing our bodies.'

'Does he intend that we should go unwashed then?' asked Charlotte, in amazement. 'I fear there would soon be very tangible feminine emanations, especially when our monthlies are on us.'

Charlotte was always the least proper of us, and Marion corrected her sharply.

'That smacks of frivolity, Charlotte, if not worse,' she said, 'and makes me even more convinced that father is right, and that we really do have need of a sterner regime than we have enjoyed heretofore.

In answer to your question, however, it is his intention that, winter and summer, we should strip and wash under the pump in the stable yard, at first dawn, before the groom arrives to take up his duties, since it would be scandalous for a male to see us in a state of nature.' She sighed. 'Now I am truly tired, and my wounded rear is paining me. I will try and give you a better idea of papa's thinking on our behalf tomorrow, but now I would be grateful if you would assist me to my room.'

We helped her to her room, and out of her clothes.

'Kneel and rest your head on your arms, Marion dear,' I said, 'and I'll fetch cloths and a basin of warm water to soothe you.'

I placed several towels under her and, as gently as I could, took her drawers carefully down and over one knee at a time, telling her to stay in that position until I had applied a soothing salve. She was in some doubt about the latter, since she felt it might not be showing proper duty to do anything that might mitigate the pain that had been inflicted for her own good. But I persuaded her it was as much to promote healthy healing, so that she could submit to proper correction the sooner, and she seemed satisfied with this.

With her drawers off, the effect of this whipping could be clearly seen. Her buttocks were a mass of overlapping bruises, some blackened from her fustigation two days since. Others were fresh, the whole extending over the lower half of her hinds, from their fullest part down to the tops of her thighs, and blending into a mass on the underside of the right buttock. There were even angry welts on the tops of her thighs, and I could not avoid speculating whether it had been these unexpected and painful cuts that had driven the screams we had heard. I did not distress my poor sister further by enquiring into the matter at that time.

Kneeling on the bed as she was, head on her pillow,

thrusting her broad but firm buttocks upwards and spreading them so that the dark divide between was opened to the viewer, I could see not only her feminine parts, but also that small wrinkled dimple adjacent. To my surprise, it was no longer so small nor dimpled. It was looking inflamed. It would seem it was not only the soreness of her thighs that caused her to walk so awkwardly, as if trying not to let those rear cheeks rub on the angry bud in between. Moreover, this pouting mouth, where her dimple had been, seemed to be slightly agape, and a thin trickle of some sticky substance descended from it onto the inside of one thigh. I did not like to mention this metamorphosis of her erstwhile rose, but let the warm cloth I was using to wash her buttocks slip into the cleft and cleanse her as gently as I could.

When we had made her as comfortable as we might, and she would allow, for she still felt it disloyal not to suffer the full consequences of her correction, she kissed us and thanked us for our kindness, but bade us finish up quickly and be sure to call her at first light, so that we could institute the new ablutional routine.

A raw and chilly dawn found us huddled in our wrappers, padding barefoot into the stable yard. Shivering already, we cast off our slight coverings and looked at each other, not sure of how to proceed. As usual Marion took the lead, as she had done since we were children.

'Charlotte, you pump vigorously and I will stand under the spout until I am quite washed all over, then Annabel shall pump for you, and I for her.'

Charlotte, naked, worked the long lever with a will, glad I think to be active in that bitter air, the water gushing from the spout in time with the rise and fall of her arms, and the swaying of her breasts. Marion loosed her long dark hair and stepped under the icy jet, turning and twisting, running her hands over her body, lifting her breasts to the chilly kiss, and parting her legs as she bent, so that the cleansing torrent reached every intimate spot. When she had doused and rubbed every part under the icy waterfall she stepped out, snatching a towel, and called for me to take over the pumping, and for Charlotte to submit herself to the arctic caress.

I too, was glad to work my shivering body while Charlotte ducked into the spouting water, squealing at the coldness of it on her bare skin, and dancing round like a heathen dervish. But Marion admonished her.

'Hush, Charlotte,' she exclaimed, 'do not make such a fuss. You are meant to be submitting your sinful body to this stimulating stream, which will help cleanse you of both your corporal foulness and the spiritual filth of sloth. For that is how papa expressed it to me, and you should attempt to endure it with the solemnity the purpose calls for.'

When Charlotte had completed her excruciating ablutions Marion dropped her towel, and came to take over the work of pumping from me. It could be seen that the cold and the icy water had brought up the marks of her corrections, so that they flamed on her white skin. Charlotte, too, showed some tracks, for she had attended papa's study two days before Marion's previous visit, but I suspected that my own hinds were comparatively lightly marked.

Papa did not like us to be without an outward and visible reminder of our imperfection, but I had last bared my buttocks for his disciplinary rod some six days ago, and the tracks were fading, helped by the fact that it had been one of his more lenient nights and I had only received eight strokes.

Gasping and hissing I stepped under the freezing jet, trying to emulate Marion's stoic behaviour, but unable to prevent some shocked cries from escaping. I washed all over, running my hands over my breasts as their nipples hardened in the icy flood, and bending low so that the jet found my rear crack and surged between my thighs, washing that part of a female body that papa, and the churchmen he never wearies of quoting, held to be the most injurious to men.

Then it was over and we all towelled ourselves vigorously to both dry ourselves and restore some circulation to our frozen limbs. As I did so, I looked up to see papa watching us from an upstairs window. He had said that it would be scandalous for a male to see us at our ablutions, but presumably he was referring to the groom and the gardener. In his case, obviously, it was his duty to check that his instruction to his erring daughters, for their better management and spiritual health, were being properly executed.

We hurried indoors to dress and open up the house, setting about the usual business of lighting fires and preparing papa's breakfast.

The morning passed without incident, but when Charlotte collected papa's luncheon tray she wore a puzzled expression, and bore a large white envelope in her hand.

'Papa says we must all put on clean drawers and then go with the groom, in the trap, to the saddler in Sexton Hinds. He will, apparently, know what papa's requirements are from the contents of this envelope.'

Needless to say, we obeyed at once, going upstairs to our rooms and changing our drawers for fresh ones in clean white cotton, which was how papa had decreed all our underwear should be.

Downstairs again we mounted into the trap, a close fit for four of us, since George the groom was a middle-aged man of broad build, and my sisters and I all well-formed young women, with adult hips.

Somehow we all fitted in, though I found it somewhat disturbing to be pressed so close to George's muscular thigh. It was nearly half-an-hour's drive to the town, and as our thighs rubbed together I became aware that George kept throwing me appraising glances which were most inappropriate to an employee. Moreover, I could not but be aware of a certain tumescence that had arisen in his breeches. I tried to withdraw, but there was no room, and my angry glances at the groom only seemed to arouse both his admiration and erection to greater heights. I bit my lip and tried to act as if unconcerned, though such was far from the case.

On arrival at Sexton Hinds George handed me down

with quite unnecessary attention, contriving in the course of it to press his rampant member against my thigh, and I could feel the pulsing length of it quite clearly through the several layers of material that, happily, separated us. I was glad when he released me, but knew it would be useless to complain to papa about George's conduct. He would reply, quite rightly, that it was the female who aroused the male and, if there was anything animal or improper in it, then the woman was the guilty party, and should be punished for so debasing the man.

I wondered if I was obliged to go to papa's study on our return, and ask him if I merited correction for affecting George so.

In the saddlers we were seen by Mr Foxis himself, who, after reading and then carefully rereading papa's letter, invited us to accompany him into a private room at the rear of his establishment. There, each of us in turn was made to sit on a bench and, utmost mortification, pull up our skirts to above the knee, exposing the bottoms of the drawers we had so recently put on. We were all most grateful to papa for his thoughtfulness in ensuring we would be spared the embarrassment of underwear in anything but pristine condition.

Mr Foxis then proceeded to take a series of careful measurements, above and below the knee, the length from knee to ankle, the girth of the ankle, and our foot sizes, our waist and wrist sizes, the circumference of our necks, the dimensions of our heads, both over the crown and around at ear level, and embarrassingly, around our bosoms and our buttocks.

17

Finally, when all that could be measured appeared to have been so, I was asked to stand with one foot on the bench and draw my skirts up onto my thigh. Blushing, I did so, then almost fell as Mr Foxis placed one end of his tape-measure on the ankle of the leg I was standing on, and slid the hand holding the other end up the length of my thigh until it pressed against my private purse, only prevented from actually making contact with my so intimate flesh by one thickness of thin cotton cloth.

My blushes redoubled, as did my gratitude to papa for ensuring that that cloth was sweet and dry, though I was surprised to find, upon returning home, that somehow the gusset had become quite moist with my secretions.

After my inside leg length had been established to Mr Foxis' satisfaction, first Charlotte and then Marion submitted to the same intimate examination and mensuration, and we ascended the trap for the journey home.

I considered asking one of the others to change places with me, so as to be spared the too intimate contact with a male limb, not to speak of the awareness of the straining member beneath the cord britches, but felt it would be selfish to avoid this embarrassment by inflicting it upon my sisters, so I steeled myself to endure George's admiring gaze and organ for the thirty minute drive home.

That evening what I had been dreading for days came to pass. I knew it was inevitable that papa would send for me soon, as he was far too considerate a guardian to neglect my discipline for long, knowing full well that the good book warns against sparing the rod and spoiling the child, and that, in this respect at least, women are in more need of correction than the most wayward child, and the most easily spoilt of God's creatures, if neglected.

I repaired to my room after supper to put on yet another pair of clean drawers, a golden rule of papa's for a daughter expecting correction, and it was then that I found the surprising fact of the wetness of the gusset.

Glad that I had not neglected my duty to put on clean apparel, thereby sparing myself further embarrassment, I went with quickening pulse and quaking belly to attend my stern superior. I was fully conscious that, if he had sent for me, I must be worthy of some punishment, or at the very least, reminder of my own frailty. But used though I was to these meetings, I still feared them and wished they were past. I sometimes wondered if I should not confess this fault to papa so that he might attempt to correct it, and make me not wish to escape my just deserts, just as Marion was inclined to refuse aid and comfort after her fustigations, on the ground that it detracted from the full benefit of the correction to the sinner.

I could feel my nipples rubbing on the coarse fabric that papa ordained for our bodices, for they had become inexplicably hard and sensitive. I believe it was fear that caused this habitual condition just prior to punishment, and despised myself for my cowardice. I resolved to show exemplary fortitude tonight, to make amends.

But despite my resolution, my hand still trembled as I knocked on that forbidding panel of oak.

On receiving permission I entered, and stood before my guardian.

He was a large, red-faced and vigorous man, at that time no more than fifty one or two, in the full flush of manhood, his florid countenance and rather heavy jowls only serving to add to his *gravitas*. He regarded me from behind his desk as I stood before it, eyes cast down, wrists crossed demurely on my belly.

'Now, miss,' he addressed me, 'it seems to me that you are, perhaps, overdue for chastisement. Would you not agree?'

What could I say but yes? To answer otherwise would not only contradict my superior, but seem to claim that I was quite free of guilt or sin these last eight days, a patent absurdity in one of my sex, and amounting to the sin of pride and arrogance in itself.

'Indeed, sir,' I said. 'It is now eight days since you helped me to overcome my failings by chastising my person.'

'And you feel that such chastisement is overdue, is that it? I seem to recall that you only received eight strokes of the cane. Would you, perhaps, consider that I was unduly lenient?'

'Sir,' I replied, 'I would not be so presumptuous. I know you have only my true interest at heart, in fustigating my weak body, and, if indeed you were a little lenient, you must have had some good reason of your own, perhaps to test my behaviour resulting from your apparent act of grace.'

'Hmm! That's as may be, child, but if I have been too easy with you, it can be corrected tonight.'

My stomach turned over, and I despised myself for failing my own resolution so soon.

'Marion will have informed you,' he continued, 'about my concern for the malign feminine influences I feel in this house, and that I intend to start a new and more strict regime to counter their ill effects. Would you say that you have any part in these deleterious emanations?'

I hesitated a moment, trying to give as honest an answer as I could to this difficult and perplexing question of the baleful effects of the female person on the male sex.

'I believe I must be guilty of some part in it, sir,' I replied, 'since I am a female with all the attributes of my sex. My figure is formed, my menses come and go regularly, and I must accept guilt. Moreover,' I added, honesty forcing me to speak, 'though I am not conscious I am exerting this baleful influence of which you speak, I was given proof of my guilt only this afternoon, when we went to Sexton Hinds, at your request.' And I told him, blushing guiltily the while, how I had been responsible for the groom's arousal.

'I fear I must have evil in me,' I said, 'for the poor man's body parts swelled up so strongly they threatened to burst through his britches, and must have caused him great discomfort, for which I should suffer an even greater punishment.'

'It is just as I thought,' he exclaimed, looking at me in sorrow. 'I have done you a great disservice, my child, leaving you to go your fatal female way, without stripes and tears to bring you back to righteousness. But, never fear, I will rectify it this very night.'

He rose from his desk and went to a cupboard I had every cause to know and fear. From the corner of my eye

21

I could see him take something long and yellow from it. I knew that cane of old. It was one of his most cruel, and stung a woman's flesh like a very viper.

'Kindly remove your drawers and mount up on the chair,' he directed, pointing to the large leather armchair with the wicked rod he held. 'I shall start by giving two dozen cuts, after which we shall decide if more should be called for. Your comportment under correction will of course have some bearing on my decision.'

Two dozen, and mounted on the chair. This was a stiff sentence, but no more than my guilty person deserved. Was I not female, and responsible for leading the groom, and who knows whom else, perhaps even my own pious father, into those sinful temptations that stir the opposite sex when the female cannot control her evil influence?

But I hated that chair, as much as I feared that rod. One had to climb up on it, with one knee on each of the padded arms. Since it was a chair of normal width, suitable for a gentleman's library, a mere woman had to spread her thighs to splitting distance to span them and then, still stretched wide open, papa insisted that we put our heads right down on the cushions of the seat, putting our arms around the chair back to support our position. It was a most testing posture, not least because it exposed all one's most intimate parts to the gaze of the chastiser and, we feared, the rod itself might even penetrate to those secret depths of our persons, now humiliatingly displayed, and wreak havoc in our soft tissues. Perhaps, in view of the dangerous nature of those parts of our female bodies to the male at this time, papa had already decided that they should be included in the portions of our anatomy to be whipped into righteousness.

With trembling hands I reached under my skirts to draw down, and discard discreetly, the thin cotton garment in which the offending parts were cased.

Then I advanced to the brooding chair on equally trembling legs, climbing first onto the seat, and hoisting my skirts clear up to my waist. Papa was very particular about this, and would award extra strokes if even one fold of cloth fell below one's narrowest portion, before swinging each knee in turn up onto the corresponding arm. I could feel the tendons at my fork stretching with the extreme parting of my thighs, and knew that my inner secrets were now visible to my guardian.

Marion and I are rather above average height for women, but despite our long lower limbs, we are only just able to spread our legs enough to place our knees in the required position, without straining the tendons in our crotches to the point where we feel the damage when we come to walk away from the place of chastisement. Charlotte has great difficulty with the position. While her limbs are well proportioned and shapely, she lacks the long thigh bones which enable Marion and I to bridge the gap between the arms, and even without the additional handicap of a bruised buttock, can only walk with a clumsy, and painful, wide-legged waddle immediately after her correction.

I bent my head and lowered it to the leather cushion that formed the seat of the dreaded chair, a process not without difficulties of its own, for we had been used to the beneficial restriction of tight lacing from the advent

23

of our womanhood, papa contending that a woman without stays was too easily led into riotous behaviour, whilst firm bones and strong laces provided a restriction on too free movement of the body that would be reflected in a similar brake on our otherwise all too weak and wandering natures. The devices he prescribed, of whalebone, steel, buckram cloth and unyielding linen lacing, extended from just below our breasts to rest on the outward jut of our buttocks behind, with a stiffened busk flattening our bellies before, and reaching down to almost the tops of our thighs, and, bending to attain the required position for this form of whipping, sent the bottom edge digging into the pad of flesh above one's pubic bone.

And now I could feel the air on those parts, and knew that the position I had assumed had opened up not only my nether cheeks, exposing my rear opening to the light, but also had made those fleshy lips that guarded my female entrance, to part, and leave all that tender tissue unprotected from either eye or rod. With my head on the seat, my shoulders were near level with my knees, and I was able to put my arms round the back of the chair, digging my fingers into the leather near the bottom of the back.

Now I was positioned correctly for the rod to have the maximum effect.

My buttocks were spread and stretched, so that the flesh was at its most vulnerable, while the confines of my position meant that I could not move one inch to avoid the worst ravages of the cane, but must hold myself steadily to absorb it. The only way I could avoid its dreadful bite would be to let my knees come off the arms, and that was unthinkable. To do so meant extra strokes, or even to take the whole punishment again the next day. On one memorable occasion Marion had slipped, I am sure it was not a voluntary movement, after twenty-three of a two dozen sentence. She was made to take the remaining stroke, then report before breakfast the next morning to take the full two dozen over again. This was the only time I ever remember Marion weeping openly after a correction, and I had no wish to follow her example. I would cling to that chair and keep my knees planted like the roots of an oak, though hell itself was loosed in my buttocks.

Papa approached and checked that my posture was correct. His hands explored my bent cheeks, probing and squeezing to assess their resilience and fitness for the cuts to come. Ordinarily he would probe my previous welts with his finger, to assess what degree of bruising remained, but on this occasion I had been left so long that only brown and green traces remained on the surface, and the swellings had all subsided to such an extent that bruising was patently absent.

His hands pressed in further to expose the fleshy parts around my 'fig', while his thumb pressed against the dimple set behind. I believe he did this to assess my general state of health, with a view to deciding how much punishment it would be reasonable to inflict.

I heard a rattle as he picked up the cane from the desk, where he had laid it while he inspected my person, and looking through the arch of my parted thighs, saw him come into my line of vision. As he raised the yellow length

25

I closed my eyes and waited, bracing my body for the first shocking blow, praying that the coming agony would help me suppress those parts of my nature that had such a harmful effect on the male sex, driving out the evil inherent in all womankind, or at least rendering it harmless.

My teeth grated as I clenched them tightly to trap my screams before they could rise, and my fingers dug even more deeply into the leather of the chair back. I was set now. The cane touched my nether cheeks, though only to mark where he would sct the first line of fire, but to my shame my flesh cringed of its own volition. Papa growled that I was clenching, and to open up. Desperately I forced my buttocks to relax, leaving them open for the rod to do its best work in the soft folds.

My heart beating wildly, I waited.

The Flesh Subdued

I had already forgotten just how deep that testing cane could bite. One might have been forgiven for thinking that with so painful an experience the memory would remain forever sharp, but I think the mind must soften the outlines of the blazing agony it raised in one's buttocks. Perhaps it was just the female mind that could perform this insidious treachery, evading thereby the lessons so assiduously imprinted in her nether parts, and intended by her master to guide her out of the paths of wrongdoing, into the way of grace. We are unruly creatures; untrustworthy, even in our own minds, and I think it quite likely that we are guilty of this evasion of our duty as of so much else.

Be that as it may, the first blow shocked me. My breath went out in a sharp cry, bitten off almost as soon as started, then returned hissing between my teeth as I felt the full flow of that throbbing agony that floods into the welt with the returning blood. Burning with shame at being so nearly undone at the first cut, I tightened my grip on the chair back, put my head even more firmly into the cushion, thrusting my spread buttocks up and back to greet the rod, and resolved to take the next stroke with better grace.

But it was impossible. If I had Marion's stoicism and bravery I might have done it, though even she had cried out last night. But I was not made of such stern stuff and, though I clung to my position nor let an outright scream pass my lips, I flinched with every cut, choked on guttural cries, and by the seventh or eighth stroke, blubbered like a child rather than the full grown woman that I was.

My guardian paused in his measured flogging of my bottom and, to my shame, admonished me for my lack of composure.

'Not only are you snivelling like a babe,' declared he, 'but you are clenching your buttocks against the rod. Loose them at once, and let the rod in. How can your soul be saved if your body will not submit?'

Mortified, I stifled my sobs and let my buttocks relax as ordered, knowing that in this fashion I would receive the utmost benefit from each stroke. Desperately I clung to the chair through ten, through twelve, through sixteen – an Andromeda clinging to her rock. But there was no Perseus with his Gorgon's head to turn the Kraken into stone. Instead the monster was in my buttocks, tearing and rending, inflicting on me the very pains of hell.

At eighteen I screamed, and nineteen too, as the cane dropped just a little to strike, not on the painful crease between buttock and thigh, but on the thigh-top itself. Papa growled his condemnation and I choked into silence, or as near to as my stertorous breath would allow. Plus the creaking of the leather as my body writhed on its perch, seemingly of its own volition and quite outside my ability to control, did not meet with papa's approval either, and he gave me another cut to my thighs to still me.

By now I had received twenty of the two dozen cuts I had been promised, and I was conscious that a desperate effort was needed to restore my credit, if further strokes on top of my present account were not to be incurred.

I dug my nails into the leather, forcing some stillness into my rebellious flesh, and set my teeth in my lip. How often had my sisters and I clung to this doleful mount in this fashion, driving our nails into the thick cowhide? So many times, in truth, that the tough skin had been all but worn through. It was only by dint of our assiduous attention, several times a week, working the best saddle soap into the hide for half-an-hour at a time, that we had managed to make it sustain our agonised assaults thus far. We tried not to think what would happen when inevitably, one of us in extremis, burst the thinning membrane. Now I was in that same extremis, literally clinging on by my fingernails to my position, and my consciousness, through the last four terrible cuts. I knew I was clenching again, for papa barked at me to make myself open, and I tried desperately to meet his requirement.

And then it was done.

The cane fell no more, and I could only lie there sobbing, conscious of how I had failed to live up to the standards I had set myself, and that papa would have wished.

I was surprised to hear the rattle of the cane as it was set down on the desk, for I was convinced that my comportment under correction had fallen far short of satisfactory.

And then I was aware of papa behind me, and something hard pressing against the little dimple set behind my softly fleeced fig. I opened my eyes, that had remained fast shut throughout, and looked through my spread thighs to see that papa's breeches were round his ankles, and he held a great throbbing member, redder than his flushed visage, directing it between my cheeks.

'Oh, papa!' I cried. 'Are you sure this is seemly?'

It cost me dear to question my father about any matter, and especially of behaviour, but the situation was so unexpected and unprecedented that I forgot my duty so far as to query his actions.

My Papa was quick to spot my fault.

'Daughter,' he gasped, for he seemed to be in the grip of some strong emotion, 'it is not for you to decide what is seemly or not. However, I will overlook your impertinence this once, though I doubt not I shall rue my softheartedness ere long, and give you an answer, though in truth you better deserve a thrashing. It would indeed be unseemly, and a cause for scandal, if I were to attempt your maidenhead. But such was never my intention for I would not wish to have you succumb to the sin of bearing a child which would damn your soul forever, and mean that I could never speak to you again, to work your salvation, nor keep you in my house.

'But know you, I am consumed with that malignant force that you and your sisters, like all women, let loose into the world, and drives men to deeds unworthy of their near divine status. For does not the book say that God has placed men near to angels, and Eve must go guilty forever? It is my intention therefore, to have you draw this poison from my system, by the suction of your rear passage, a foul receptacle for a foul discharge, and of the utmost appropriateness since you must bear the responsibility for

30

its upsurgence in the first place. You may well find it causes you pain. Accept that pain into your body and give thanks that you are privileged to bear it, while you go some way to right the wrong you have caused me, and all men.'

My father's words overwhelmed me with their force and wisdom, and obediently I submitted myself to his advances, happy to have been given this opportunity to make amends for my evil effect on him, and offer up the sacrifice of my pain in expiation.

I think he must have anointed his manly weapon when he went back to his desk, for besides being bright red, it glistened with some oily substance, which was another proof of his wisdom as, without it, he would have been hard put to it to have penetrated me.

As it was he hurt me considerably as he forced the head past my sphincter ring, adding to my discomfort by his steely grip on my so recently flogged buttocks. I could not but cry out in shocked gasps as he forced me deeper, until his belly, with its covering of coarse hair, was rubbing on those same tender welts. I wondered how to suction the venom from his loins, but he solved the problem for me by pulling his great rod most of the way out of my bowel, before thrusting it back in up to the hilt.

I soon learnt to contract my belly, and my sphincter, as he withdrew, relaxing them again to ease his re-entry, an action similar I believe to that of milking a cow's teat. I seemed to have made a satisfactory choice of behaviour for very shortly his motion quickened, his breath became shorter, as the venom tried to resist my efforts to extract it, and then I felt the foulness leave his body and spurt in hot jets into my unworthy belly.

I felt proud and grateful to have been of such service to my papa, though I must admit, a trifle sore. But what was that compared with the good I had been privileged to do?

I was even more certain of my good fortune in being able to render this assistance to my parent, when I sensed the magnitude of the relief he enjoyed in being freed from that hateful feminine contagion. So great it was that he collapsed, quite overcome, onto my back, and lay there panting with his new found peace of mind. I gladly bore his weight until he came to himself enough to rise and adjust his dress. Well satisfied with my work I waited, as in duty bound, until dismissed, before attempting to rise myself.

I had always found it presented some difficulty, getting down from the chair and assuming my drawers, since one's welts made for painful bending, and even the touch of the thin cotton fabric could be uncomfortable where the skin was particularly abraded.

But now I found myself suffering additionally, from the inflamed state of my anus. Though dear papa had shown great consideration in greasing that portion through which the evil essence had been drawn out, the procedure had abraded the ring of my sphincter, and it was painful when the cheeks of my buttocks closed on it. As I made an awkward exit, my legs shuffling in a curious gait, I recognised the way Marion had moved the night before, and it dawned on me that she, too, had been granted the boon of drawing out the foulness that sapped papa's strength and spirituality.

I was not jealous. Marion and I have always been close and shared everything, so why not this? I did not think Charlotte had yet been so privileged, but would welcome her as an equal when her time came. In the meantime, I resolved, this should be a secret between Marion and I. It would be unfair to let Charlotte know what rewarding service she was missing.

I dragged myself to my room and, presently, Marion and Charlotte came by to render me the same service that Marion had received the previous night. I must, however, admit with feelings of guilt, that I made no move to deflect the comforting applications of cold compresses, warm flannels, and emollient creams, that my dear sisters used to mitigate my sufferings. I am but a weak vessel compared to Marion, and backslider that I am, took no care that I should feel my chastisement to the last degree, as a truly repentant female should.

As Marion's hand gently drew a warm and soapy flannel through the divide of my buttocks, wiping away the ooze from my anus, she and I exchanged looks that told each other of our understanding, and mutely made compact to leave Charlotte ignorant of the nature of our hidden service, until her own time came to partake.

For the next few days our daily routine, including the freezing douche under the stable pump each dawn, continued to take its usual course including, naturally, a summons for Charlotte to attend on papa, two evenings after my own visit, for she had last been corrected about seven days before, and papa held that a woman left unwhipped for more than a week had fallen so far into the devil's clutches that she could only be reclaimed by such a flogging as to render her unable to ease her soul by full and proper labour, and he had too much affection for his daughters to risk the need to subject them to such a deprivation.

When Charlotte returned from her correction she seemed in some distress of mind, as well as of body. It did not take long to discover that she had been disconcerted by papa's need to use her buttocks to draw out the troubling matter in his body. I saw then the infinite wisdom of our protector, in choosing to confer the privilege of such service on Marion and myself first, before offering Charlotte the same benison. Our middle sister had always been the slowest to understand the deeply religious and philosophical basis for the disciplines we lived under, and by making us privy to his thinking first, he was able to ensure that we would be able, and from experience, to explain to our slower sister the benefits we both conferred, and had conferred on us in return. By the time we had treated her hurts, and soothed her sores, Charlotte was able to accept the truth of what he taught as readily as we did ourselves.

Two days later we saw the first results of our visit to the saddler, a visit whose purpose had escaped us up until now. A boy on a pony delivered a package, which Marion took straight to papa. When she returned a little later she still bore the package, although now it had been opened, presumably so that papa could satisfy himself that the contents were as he prescribed.

Marion invited us to remove our drawers, reaching down at the same time to draw off, and discard, her own. Reaching into the package she drew out, and distributed, three sets of curious restraints. Each consisted of a pair of leather lined steel bands, joined by a short length of chain. Each band was engraved with an M, an A, or a C, to identify the wearer for whom it was intended, and I remembered that Mr Foxis had measured us most particularly round every conceivable part of our bodies.

Marion explained.

It appeared that papa had consulted with various learned friends on the troublesome effects of the female presence in a house of Godliness, and had been advised, amongst other things, to reduce our physical mobility as far as was compatible with allowing us the beneficial influence of hard work on our domestic duties.

'Papa said,' she went on, 'that all the authorities agree it is lack of restraint that contributes most to the waywardness of women and, hence, to the debilitation and degradation of men they come into contact with. We are therefore to clasp the bands around our lower limbs, just below the knee, where we garter our stockings. The chain will then ensure we do not betray our womanhood by striding like a man, or running at any time.'

We each donned our allotted restraint, and tried the effect of walking. It was possible, with care, to walk fairly freely about the kitchen, simulating the performance of typical duties, but one's progress was slow unless one made very rapid steps.

Ascending stairs was an entirely different matter, and at first we were baffled by the problem. But a little trial and error soon taught us that, by turning one knee in against the other, that foot could be swung up onto the first step, and the process repeated either with the same foot or its companion, and the stairs might be negotiated fairly readily, but with either a halting step or a strange twisting motion. No matter, we would be able to provide papa with his meals in his room, and those other services we were learning to render him, and reach our own bedrooms too.

It appeared that papa intended that we should wear these devices day and night, hence the removal of our drawers, and that we would no longer have any need for such garments in the future. Apparently one of his learned friends, a medical man, was of the opinion that a woman's genitals should be kept open to the air, for health and sanitation, though a napkin might be worn when our time of the month was on us.

The saddler had done a fine job of measuring and manufacture, and the bands clasped us firmly, but not so tightly as to interfere with circulation. The leather was soft, thick, and had rounded edges so as not to chafe us, though we found that with continuous use they did dig into our flesh a little, especially if we forgot the humble gait that had been impressed upon us, and brought ourselves to a jarring stop by overstepping the length of chain.

The bands were closed by pushing one end into a slot in

a boss formed on the rear. When the ends were fully home an internal spring-catch engaged, and the band could not be removed without cutting through it; an almost impossible task for us, the band being tempered steel and we bereft of locksmiths' tools.

Not that we have attempted such a violation of our father's command to wear them day and night, but it was somehow comforting to know that, even away from his presence, he had actual physical control of our persons. I think we all basked in an added feeling of security as we tested our new fetters. We even welcomed the fact that they were steel, and would require to be regularly scoured to keep them rust free and shining, especially after our outdoor ablutions, the sense of participating in our own restraint adding to our proper feelings of submission.

That evening we were all summoned to papa's study. It was one of those rare occasions when no one of us was subjected to his rod. He contented himself with having us draw our skirts up to our thighs so that he could inspect our newly acquired curbs, checking them for tightness and security, and having us move about to demonstrate the limits on our mobility.

We settled into our established routine, although a slightly different pattern was emerging. We found ourselves summoned to receive papa's guidance, and relieve his troubled spirit, on a more regular basis, each of us being required to attend him at weekly intervals, and in the order of our births.

I do not know which was more trying for our nerves; the uncertainty that had prevailed before, or the near certainty that one could predict one's correction and service to the day.

It was not long before the saddler's efforts bore further fruit. Soon we found ourselves wearing high collars, constructed on the same principles as those below our knees, but of such a width that they fitted from the collarbone to the jaw-line, where a roll edge ensured we were not too severely chafed. But we were obliged to keep our chins up and our heads held high. It was providential that our fetters were delivered some time in advance of the collars, as we had had some time to master the art of placing our feet on rough ground while constrained to tiny steps. And more particularly, we had perfected the mode of ascending stairs by turning in one knee against the other, and could manage it competently without the need to look down, which the collars, of course, made quite impossible.

On one occasion, Charlotte had the temerity to make some remark to papa about the apparent biblical condemnation of the stiff-necked. She was still inclined to behave in a somewhat froward fashion, and papa, I believe, did her no service by occasionally indulging her. On this occasion, however, he rebuked her for her questioning of his judgement in the matter, and ordered her to attend him the next night – that evening already reserved for myself – even though it was but three days since she had last been corrected, and that severely. She dropped her eyes in submission, though her chin was still held firmly aloft.

Gradually his plan for us, based on his own fine intellect

and the advice of those wise and learned friends he consulted, unfolded before us. His intent to keep our femininity in check while maintaining our availability for labour and service, also included certain devices to be worn about our persons. These would constantly impinge upon our flesh in such a way as to keep us reminded of our corporal weaknesses and cleanse our minds to think, as much as women can, of spiritual things.

Though not really a High Churchman, he professed to a great admiration for some of the enclosed orders of nuns. Especially the more strict Spanish convents, and their solution to the problem of the uncleanness of women and their contagion of men, by rigid discipline and regular mortification of the flesh.

To this end he had commissioned from the saddler several more useful items. Firstly we were each given a saddle strap to wear. This consisted of another reinforced belt, fitting as snugly round our waists as our other gear about our necks and knees. From it depended a chain, which was passed through the legs, the lips of our vulvas being parted to receive it the more deeply, then drawn up between our rear cheeks to snap into a fastening at the rear of the belt. When the fastening was pushed home to the last click of the locking spring, the chain cut deep into our softest parts.

The device served its purpose admirably, and in more than one way. In the first place, of course, we were given that constant reminder of our flesh, for the chain cut in quite hard enough to cause us soreness from the start, and after some hours wearing it, this would have accumulated to a degree that could not easily be ignored, but must nevertheless be endured.

Then, as we moved even the short steps dictated by our fetters, the chain would move in our creases, sawing even more severely at our soft woman's parts.

Again, we had to wear these cinches day and night, even when performing our natural functions, and it may be imagined the real mortification we suffered, the chain between our legs, and especially over our anuses, ensuring we would soil ourselves most times we made to relieve the pressure in our bowels or bladders.

And so life went on for us three young women, cradled in the security of our bondage, starting each day invigorated by our duckings beneath the pump, which effectively guarded us from the misery of sloth, our souls and bodies kept on that strait and narrow path that leads to salvation, by close restraint and mortification of our most intimate flesh, and basking in the knowledge that we were storing up treasure in heaven by our good works, our care of God's minister, and the easing of his troubled spirit.

Nor was he the only male whose potentially debilitating fluids we drew out. A week or so later I attended papa's study, in the course of the rota that had been established, and was astounded to find another man, besides my parent, in the room with him.

I stammered my apologies for disturbing them and made to withdraw, but papa recalled me.

'Come here, child,' he instructed, 'and prepare yourself.'

'But papa,' I stammered, 'do you intend that I should

bare myself in front of a stranger, a male person?'

'Ungrateful wretch, do you forget you duty so far as to question your own father?' he exclaimed. 'You see the unruly nature I have to overcome, sir,' he went on, addressing the tall black figure of his visitor, 'and why only the strictest discipline will suffice.'

'Indeed, sir,' the latter replied, in a deep and penetrating voice that somehow caused my stomach to quake. 'I will bear that in mind, when advising you on further measures you might adopt.'

Papa turned his attention back to my quaking self. 'This is Dr Boucher, a physician with a special knowledge of the female and all her problems and dangers. I have invited him here to advise me on what measures are best for the proper management of you and your sisters, and the maintenance of your health, both physical and mental.'

He bestowed on me a quelling look.

'There can be no possible objection to a medical man attending while you bare your person, and he will indeed need to do so in order to give you that physical examination he holds necessary for him to give his professional opinion on your present state of health, and ability to sustain such disciplinary measures as shall, from time to time, be prescribed. Now place yourself in your proper position on the chair, and let us have no more nonsense.'

I dropped a curtsey, as much as my knee fetters would allow, by way of acknowledgement and apology, and hastened to obey. I could feel the blushes rising to my cheeks as I gathered up my skirts to my waist, feeling the air, and the visitor's eyes on my other cheeks and the

41

feminine secret between.

Mounting the chair seat in fetters presented some difficulty, and my struggles to ascend the cushion of the seat was, I fear, rather lacking in dignity, and I hoped I was not shaming papa in front of his guest. I waited there, with my skirts on the small of my back, while papa released the band from my right knee. Then I lifted it to place it on the arm that side, then the left knee onto the other arm with the loose end of my cincher chain dangling between my legs, spreading me widely in the pose that had by now become standard for our corrections.

'Perhaps,' said papa, addressing the good doctor, 'it might be as well if you were to make a full examination of the subject before we proceed further, or at least, of those parts that will be most directly involved in this evening's discipline and reparation. Though she is the youngest of my daughters she is as well formed as her elder sisters, and I doubt not that you will find her fully equipped to sustain salutary punishment and draw forth those evil essences that the unwholesomeness of the female presence is instrumental in causing to rise and fester in men.'

If any proof were needed of the shameful folly of women, it was there, for my vanity was such that I actually glowed to hear my father describe my person in such terms. I tried to think if my reaction was due simply to pride. Or was it satisfaction that I should give him cause to think well of me? I found that I could easily resolve this dilemma by applying the golden rule, that papa never tired of propounding, that if in two minds as to whether a woman's actions arose from commendable, or uncommendable motives, it was always safest to assume the latter.

The good doctor made no demur and, instantly it seemed, I became aware of hands on my spread buttocks, palping the rounded cheeks, not as free to move in their bent position, and prodding with strong bony fingers to assess their firmness. Then the fingers stroked down the valley between my nether cheeks, finding the anus and probing it gently, testing the bud and tracing its circumference. Despite the fact that he was in no way rough, I flinched, for I was still sore from the effect of the chain on a tender gland that had been entered by my father's member only four days before, for Marion had been on her monthlies and I had taken her place in the rota for the easing of papa's distension. Although, thankfully, he had not suggested that I should take the strokes due to her on that occasion.

Now the doctor transferred his attention, and his fingers, to those parts between my thighs, below the soft covering of dark fur at the base of my belly. They parted the fleshy lips, already a little agape by virtue of my spread thighs, and touched gently around the opening that led to my womb.

A fingertip carefully tested the membrane of my maidenhead, eliciting an interested 'mm'. And then it travelled up to that little bud above, that we girls used to ease our own, and each others, deepest tensions and distresses, especially after correction, though we sometimes felt some guilt at thus avoiding the ultimate in benefit from the rod's application and, indeed, Marion would usually refuse this benison, except when she was in so much distress that she was beyond exercising her usual influence on Charlotte and I, and, despite her reservations, we would ease the screaming of her nerves and lower her gently into sleep.

Now the doctor's finger was performing that same circular dance that we used on those occasions, and I could feel the blood rushing to it, and the little member hardening and rising. The doctor's tongue made 'tsk tsk', whether in disapproval of my reaction or interest in the organ and its behaviour I could not say, and then he withdrew.

'You are right, sir,' he said, addressing papa. 'She is, indeed, a very well formed young female.'

I blushed again at the vanity I felt surge in me, and wondered if duty did not require me to confess this sin to papa, so that it might be added to the tally of the strokes I was to receive. But I was distracted from this question of conscience by the doctor continuing.

'The buttocks are particularly fine,' he declared, 'without being in any way overlarge, and their underlying musculature is overlaid with just sufficient fatty tissue that you may anticipate no harm coming to it from even the most severe and prolonged thrashing. I note that the anus is somewhat inflamed, but I think it can sustain considerable further usage before there is any major risk of substantial haemorrhoid formation. Should this happen, and their degree and nature interfere with the functions for which it is to be used, then I would recommend cauterisation, but we are a long way from having to face that possibility.'

'I am gratified to hear it,' replied papa, 'for it would be most inconvenient to be deprived of her services for any length of time. How did you find her other parts?'

'I can report that, as you trusted and hoped, the hymen is still intacta. It is a sound healthy membrane, and should survive until required by a suitable mate. The restriction of the thighs should help to ensure that it is not stretched to rupture in the course of daily activities, but you must take care when using the arms of the chair for a whipping stand, as I fear it will be under considerable tension. I suggest the young woman be warned very clearly that serious consequences would arise should she not control herself properly under correction, and any movement lead to a fall and loss of hymen.'

'She is already aware of that fact,' papa growled, with a touch of menace in his voice that made me tremble a little on my perch.

'I'm glad to hear it,' the doctor replied. 'Now, as to the clitoris, it is a generous but not overlarge organ, quite sensitive and erectile.'

'Very good, sir,' said papa. 'Now, I propose we proceed to the correction of this erring female bent in front of us. I take it that your findings would be quite consistent with the infliction of a dozen strokes of the cane, the normal sum for these occasions, plus any extras due for specific transgressions.'

'Oh, yes, this buttock could sustain many times that number without other than superficial, or at least only subcutaneous, injury. No damage to bone or tendon, I assure you.'

'Good. I see from my book that she is not in fact due any extra on this occasion,' my spirits rose, prematurely as it happened, 'but there is the little matter of her objection to your presence on entering the room. Three extra would appear consistent with justice and proper discipline and, as the offence was in some sense against yourself, I suggest it would be appropriate if you were to deliver the strokes yourself.'

'I shall be glad to assist you in the matter,' came the reply. 'And it will also give me an opportunity to test the elasticity of the buttock under the rod, at first hand.'

'Let us proceed then,' said papa. 'Annabel, my child, do lower your head to the cushion, and thrust out your haunches. You know well how to hold your buttocks for the cane. Let me see you hold them so for the benefit of the good doctor, and for the better correction of your sinful nature.'

Ever obedient to my papa, I lowered my head to the cushion, a task made more uncomfortable now with the advent of our stiff high collars, and clasped the chair back in my arms. Biting my lip in concentration I willed my buttocks to relax, feeling the cleft behind spread itself like an opening flower, revealing my anus and the gaping vulva below. I would not fail papa. This visitor, apparently of such consequence, should see me offer myself wholly for the coming correction, though inwardly I quaked and my stomach filled with nauseous fear.

Church, Medicine & the Law

I had never been corrected in the presence of anyone other than papa, let alone a member of the male sex and, though it caused me some shame to be seen thus, naked, my bare buttocks spread, revealing my most intimate female parts, it also roused me to steel myself and offer my body to the rod without reservation, inviting the utmost of each stroke and honouring my parent, by demonstrating that his care of us had not been without fruit and, though still mere women, we had at least learnt the virtues of obedience and fortitude.

Although it was an ordeal to which I had many times been subjected, a flogging of a dozen strokes with that penal rod was still something of dread, and I could look forward to three more besides from the doctor, whose athletic build and wiry wrists gave promise of cuts at least as searching as those that papa was about to unleash on my unprotected buttocks.

I closed my eyes, bit my lip, and set myself not only to endure, but to endure with honour.

As the first cut sank into my flesh I bit down on my lip so hard that I could taste blood, but I held my pose and made no more noise than a grunt buried deep in my throat. I knew too well from experience that the first stroke is always worse than one's worst imaginings, and I was determined not to be caught out and lose the battle at the first engagement. Breathing heavily through my nose, I rode out the appalling pain in my behind and set myself for the next, with a little more courage.

Though the second was every whit as bad, it was that little easier to master for having ridden the first. To have lost there is so discouraging that it saps one's strength. Now I could give my attention to keeping my flesh open to the correction, and accepting its formative anguish into my body without flinching or crying out.

I could not hope to wholly succeed, of course. Perhaps Marion could have endured to the end, but she is braver than I and, moreover, of some seven years more maturity. But twelve cuts of that awful rod seem, eventually, to penetrate to one's very soul, each one like a hand twisting that poor weak female thing until it screams inside one. As it is, I hope I did not disgrace papa, for I only cried out from the seventh stroke, which caught me lower than I had been expecting. The shock was such that I involuntarily clenched behind, and papa had to speak sharply to me to get me to open up my buttocks again.

For the rest of my dozen I fought hard to hold them relaxed and spread, but it is well known that, once the dam has burst, it is difficult to keep the waters pent up, and I could not entirely suppress the screams that rose to my throat while my tears were quite unconfined.

When the last of the dreadful dozen had ebbed down for the unbearable agony of its flood, papa handed the yellow cane to the doctor, asking, 'And what is your opinion now, sir?'

'I think she does you credit, sir,' the man of healing

replied. 'Quite commendable fortitude for the first half, though there is still scope to train her to endure further. Certainly her flesh will go a great deal further.'

'Very well,' my father seemed quite pleased with this reply, 'perhaps you would lay on the extra trio she earned at your expense.'

I had somewhat recovered myself in the respite afforded by this exchange, and determined to set up my defences once again. But I had reckoned without the doctor who, I learnt later, had much experience of female correction and the means of breaking their resistance. At measured intervals, spaced so that I was caught at the crest of the proceeding wave by the new cut searing into my flesh, he drove three excruciating strokes into my thighs, just an inch below that soft crease that divided the rounded resilience of my buttocks from my legs. I shrieked in protest, digging my nails into the leather of the chair and, after the last, my head came up, quite beyond my control, and I howled like a bitch.

I had expected papa to order immediate and condign retribution, but it would seem that he was either too affected by that female contamination, or so involved with his scientific collaboration with the good doctor, for he neglected me shamefully, offering no correction for my fall from grace, and proceeded at once to the next usual act, namely the penetration of my anus by his male member, so that I could redeem myself in some measure by assisting in the drawing off of the poison in his system.

On this occasion he was more rough and vigorous than usual, and I cried out more than once as his belly slammed into my sore buttocks, and my tender sphincter was pulled almost to inversion by his rapid out takes. But I did my duty and clenched on his shaft, as I had learnt to do with the muscles of both my belly and my anal sphincter.

It seemed no time at all before I had accomplished my object, and I felt the debilitating substance that had been troubling him so greatly, puffing up his male organ, ejected into my rectum in great hot spurts.

I have to admit that I was somewhat fatigued after this exercise, and lay resting my cheek on the back of the chair, awaiting permission to descend.

But my duties were not quite over, however.

Papa left me on my awkward mount while he recovered somewhat, then heaved himself off my back, adjusting his breeches as he addressed the doctor.

'As you may see, sir, the process of extraction is quite quickly accomplished, and most efficacious. I am aware of the benefit already. Now I know you have a household full of women, and you must, yourself, suffer badly from the same complaint, and the infection can only have been exacerbated by your close proximity to my daughters, for I fear that they are a particularly virulent source of these noxious effusions.

'For your own relief, and in the interest of scientific investigation, of course,' he added, smoothing down his waistcoat and adjusting his buttons, 'you should essay the passage yourself, and see how beneficial it can be.'

Almost at once I felt another hard rod against my sphincter. I braced myself against the coming pain, though I knew now not to clench my buttocks, but to strain outwards as if answering a call of nature, as soon as the head was pressed into the anus. It was with great relief that I found that papa's discharge, combined with the remains of the grease with which he had customarily anointed his member, led to a less painful entry than my first impalement of the evening.

I dutifully worked on the doctor's excess of female contamination and, in a gratifyingly short time, was able to effect complete relief. But what with the effort and discomfort I had suffered, and was still suffering, I was almost insensible by the time the doctor had finished his rest on my back, and had to be helped to my feet, after the doctor had carried out a further examination and pronounced me only temporarily exhausted, and having taken no injury that a healthy young woman, such as myself, could not throw off in a very short space of time.

After papa had refastened the band about my right knee, so as to restore those restraints on my impetuosity judged so necessary for the proper management of women, I made shift to drag myself to my room. But my halting shuffle took me little further than the outside of papa's door, where I was found by my loving sisters and helped to my bed.

While they bathed my wounded buttocks, for the doctor's cuts, though not as numerous as papa's, were on skin that had not become accustomed, by usage, to bearing the rod and, consequently, had come up instantly into thick purple ropes, I told them of this new departure, and how there had been a stranger present at my correction.

Charlotte, ever ready to speak without that due consideration and respect for the actions of men, was quick to exclaim that it was not proper, but Marion hushed her while I finished the tale, explaining his profession, and papa's reasons for engaging him to examine us.

Charlotte was most abashed to hear how mistaken and undutiful she had been to have doubted papa's discretion in the matter and agreed, albeit a little reluctantly I thought, to Marion's suggestion that she should purge her conscience by confessing her fault to papa at the earliest opportunity, so that it might be entered in his book and accounted for at her next correction. This was to be in four days' time, as Marion was scheduled next, in two days.

On that occasion, too, as might be expected given papa's intention to have a medical opinion on each of us, and a scientific assessment of how to proceed with our management, Dr Boucher attended the correction, and made an informed inspection of Marion's nether parts, giving it as his opinion, *inter alia*, that she too was a well formed female, who could bear severe and extended correction if called for.

Papa had decreed that she should receive six extra strokes for having failed to keep her previous appointment, on account of her menses, and these he allocated to the doctor, who laid half on the already twelve times striped buttock, and three, as in my own case, to the tops of her thighs.

I think it must have been in the interests of investigating our physiological responses to trauma, that he chose this rather unusual site for the welts he laid on our persons, for a few days later he performed exactly the same service for Charlotte, who was awarded three extra for her self-confessed lack of respect for her parent's judgement in introducing a male into our discipline sessions, which, as with Marion and myself, he laid on her thighs, rather than her buttocks.

Charlotte was also the subject of an intense intimate examination, and reported that Dr Boucher had diagnosed her form as well suited to the rod and extended correction, as we others. Apparently he considered her clitoris as, 'Not of unreasonable size for a healthy woman, though probably rather more sensitive than some.'

The doctor continued to be a regular visitor to our house, and papa prevailed on us to offer him our services for the draining of his unwholesome, and feminine inspired, gatherings of fluid, for it appeared he was constantly surrounded by females in his practice and his household.

I did make so bold as to enquire of papa, whether one of these ladies might not be prevailed upon to do him this service, though I made it clear we were very sensible of the honour he did us by choosing our company. Papa answered, rather shortly, that the good doctor's undutiful wife had not only refused him this service, but expressly forbidden any of the other women of the household to perform it. Papa turned the conversation elsewhere, but I think he was trying to spare us this embarrassment of hearing of one of our sex who was so lost to decency as to refuse any request of the man to whom she owed her total and unquestioning obedience.

Not many days later we were joined by yet another visitor. Although we should have known better, after our ridiculous and unfilial doubts when papa brought Dr Boucher into the house at times of correction, we had learnt no better, and protested our dismay.

Again we found ourselves rebuked by our parent, more in sorrow for our lack of trust and obedience, than in anger, although he did not neglect to punish us for it after. It seems the gentleman was none other than Lord Justice Rodsham, a celebrated disciplinarian, and who more suitable to observe and advise on such quasi-judicial and penitential business as our correction and control?

Our visitors did not only come on nights when one of us was to be corrected, but might call at any time to make use of our expertise in relieving the deadly matter gathering in their bodies from the too baleful influence of the females whose proximity they could not avoid.

Usually we were not chastised on these intermediate visits, and we were grateful that there was this spreading of the burden for, truth to tell, we all three found it rather demanding of our women's bodies to have to relieve three men, one after the other, in the weakened state we were often in, subsequent to receiving twelve or more strokes of papa's searching rod on our constantly bruised buttocks.

Now that we were receiving two visitors regularly, as well as keeping papa's tensions in check, one or other of us would unloose her chain, most nights, and offer her anal services.

It was obvious that all three men had spent long in too close contact with contaminating femininity, and that their fate would be unhappy indeed without the care we were able to lavish on them. And it occurred to me to wonder how they had managed, before we had stepped into the breach, or rather, they into ours.

I did not know it then, it only became apparent later, but they had in fact, all three, been in the habit of visiting a widow of the district, who had rendered them similar remedial treatment to that we supplied. Unfortunately, a month or so before the period of which I speak, some ladies of the county had banded together to denounce the widow for immodest behaviour, citing her low cut bodices when attending divine service, that barely covered her nipples, her lustrous hair, on which she set no more than a scrap of lace and, horror of horrors, her way of gathering her skirts, so that not only her foot, in its delicate kid boot, was visible, but even her ankle and a glimpse of embroidered stocking.

So indignant were the ladies that they were able to prevail on a local magistrate not only to have her charged with indecent behaviour, but to find her guilty as charged and sentence her to be whipped through the town, from Eastgate to Westgate and back to the market place, where she was to spend two hours in the pillory before being drawn, naked, on a hurdle to Buttock Cross on the county boundary, and there sent on her way under threat of transportation if she ever appeared in the town again.

As it happens, we had witnessed her downfall, though we had no knowledge of the true circumstances, for that very market day, papa, ever careful for our good, had suddenly declared his intention to take us all to Sexton

Hinds, to equip us with new supplies of cotton drawers, which he had recently decided should be our constant wear.

On approaching the town we found the main street thronged with people, apparently waiting for some event. They made to part and let us through on the way to the drapers, where we were to have our new undergarments selected for us, but papa declared the press would frighten our horse, and he would hold back until the crowd dispersed. I was somewhat surprised at this, since the horse was of the most sanguine disposition, and could be driven through a howling mob without changing its pace one jot, but papa seemed to have his mind quite made up to stay, and I held my peace, as a good daughter should.

Presently, the crowd starts to bay and cheer behind us, and we turned to see a cart approaching very steadily down the centre of the street. The crowd parted to let it pass, then closed behind it, cheering and waving. As it got nearer we could see that the cart was followed by a woman of about five or six and thirty years. She was naked to the waist, the bodice of her gown torn down until it rested in tatters on her flaring hips, and she was constrained to follow the cart unwaveringly, by reason that her wrists were tied fast to the tailgate. She wore no stays, and her large breasts hung on her chest heavily. When younger she must have been quite a beauty; her waist was still narrow, her bare feet, peeping out beneath her kilted gown small and delicate, and her features still smooth with good bones, though her face was distorted by the extreme emotion she was under, for, as she was forced by the slow and even progress of the cart to walk equally slowly down the street, the brutal figure of the town jailer marched behind her, and at every second pace brought a vicious black whip down across her back and shoulders.

Left, right, left, crack, her calvary proceeded, gasping at each blow, crying out and twisting when a particularly cruel lash curled round her flank and bit in under her arm, where the flesh is tenderest. When she twisted, her large and slightly pendulous breasts swung violently on her heaving chest like, as Charlotte so crudely remarked, 'turnips in a sack'. Her nudity was made all the more bizarre by the fact that she was completely bald. It appeared that, though she had once been proud of her lustrous dark locks, it was customary to cut them off, to leave the back bare to the whip, and her head bobbed behind the cart, shaved clean all over, another smooth turnip to match those swinging on her chest.

After the cart and its doleful followers had passed, papa drew our trap into the road, and made shift to follow as far as the marketplace, where we watched as the wretch was cut down from the cart.

She had to be supported, gasping and sobbing, to the pillory, where her wrists and neck were gripped by the cut-outs in the sturdy timbers, and the top lowered, leaving her to face the mocking crowd, unable to use her hands to cover her face or deflect the missiles, for the crowd was making great sport, and threw all manner of filth and rotten eggs, from which she was quite unable to defend herself.

Foremost among her attackers were a group of finely dressed women, who I judged to be the wives of burgesses of the town, or yeomen farmers of the district. Some openly jeered at the poor woman, and purchased ancient eggs and rotten cabbages from the hucksters peddling them to all who would pay, and others of the heartless band, too nice to do such work themselves, slipping coins to rough men and coarser women in the throng, to purchase similar fare or worse and throw it on their behalf. I saw one offer a slattern a shilling if she would throw the fresh steaming dung our horse let drop into the widow's unprotected face and shaven pate.

Nor was it only her head and face that suffered, for the pillory below the cross planks was but a post little more than a hand's breath across, and gave no shelter from the furious rain of filth. As much was aimed at her breasts and belly as her visage, and she was fouled over every part.

When the commotion had died down somewhat, papa completed our journey to the draper's shop, and ushered us all in. The woman who was the proprietor had been advised of our coming, and papa's wants, and had ready for us several sizes and patterns of drawers or pantaloons.

Papa first had us line up and lift our gowns right up to our waists, leaving ourselves quite bare below, for we had not put on anything at his instruction. The shopkeeper then assisted us into each of her styles, until papa had made his choice for us, and then each of us assumed the chosen style in several sizes until he was quite satisfied.

When it was all over we each had three pairs of serviceable drawers, chosen by papa to be well fitting on our rounded posteriors, but a loose fit along the length of our thighs, almost to the knee.

All this choosing and fitting had taken a great deal of time, extended by the tea and cakes for which papa had rather uncharacteristically sent, in such good mood he was, and by the time we emerged from the draper's shop with our purchases the crowd was re-gathering, for the widow's two hours were up and she was to be drawn to the county boundary, and sent packing.

Before she was released from the frame in which she was trapped by her head and hands, the jailer went behind her and cut the waistband of her gown, drawing it to the ground. The woman cried and protested as her lower portions were uncovered, but the jailer ignored her sobs and entreaties, for the sentence was that she should be drawn naked.

While he stripped her roughly, I noticed that several of the same well dressed women, who had ensured she suffered at the hands of the filth throwers, had stayed to see her further humiliated, and added their own shrill invective to the howls of the mob.

The now naked woman was taken down from the pillory, scarce able to stand, and it could be seen that she was as well formed below, as above. Her legs were long and straight, the thighs well rounded without being overly plump, and the joint of her thighs supporting a thick bush of glossy thatch, no doubt matching the luxurious tresses of which she had been shorn before being flogged.

Now a crude hurdle was brought, and the woman laid on it on her back, causing her to cry out anew. Her arms were parted to secure her wrists to the top corners of the wattle frame, and her legs drawn apart, to lash her ankles to the lower corners. Spread like a starfish, her parts were open for all to see. Her widely spread thighs left her nether lips gaping at the beholders, revealing even the delicate inner folds, with her bud, which was very large and prominent, clearly showing at the top.

A horse was harnessed to the hurdle and commenced to draw it, and its white and weeping burden, towards the Westgate, and papa made haste to follow.

Once again we followed as the horse was driven, at a smart trot now, along the mired and cobbled street, the naked woman receiving a fresh coating of ordure from the evidence of horse and cattle in the street, while the bouncing of her bare and beaten flesh on the rough woven sticks of the hurdle must have caused her excruciating torment.

The small procession of the horse with its postillion, ourselves, and several other conveyances, including one containing several of the vindictive ladies of fashion we had previously observed, revelling in the widow's sufferings, proceeded for over a mile until we reached Buttock Cross, where a weathered pillar bearing the faint remains of a carved cross, marked the boundary in the midst of a barren moor.

The woman was cut free of her painful carriage, but at first could scare stand, so weakened and exhausted was she. The harpies who had followed her so far, called her harlot and bid her be gone, and, when she seemed not to hear them, called on the postillion who had drawn her to the place of parting to send her on her way, which he did, uncoiling the long thin whip he carried and lashing the poor naked form until she set off down the road, away from her home and erstwhile friends, stumbling and limping, her hands clasped round her breasts, her shoulders heaving with her sobs.

The party watched her until she disappeared in a dip in the road, then turned and went their different ways.

One cannot but feel some compassion for the lady, for had she not worked unselfishly to ease the throbbing excesses of poisonous matter generated in several worthy men of the district? But we did not know that at the time. In any case, had she not displayed blatant indecency, and in a place of worship, as well as the public thoroughfare. Several witnesses at the trial, including many of the ladies most vociferous in their condemnation of her at her flogging, had testified how, passing her kneeling in her pew, they had looked down and seen her rosy nipples peeping through the lace of her bodice, and had had to interpose themselves so that their husbands or sons might not be offended by the sight.

And others claimed to have seen the whole of a kid leather boot, replete with a dozen brass buttons, which her shortened skirts revealed as she descended the steps outside, after service. Such indelicacy is not to be borne in any well-regulated community, and no doubt I am at fault in sympathising with the woman at all.

In any event, she left the district, and it was from that time that our regime became more 'tight' and our discipline more rigid.

The new drawers, that had been the pretext for our visit to Sexton Hinds the day the widow was whipped through the streets, had little use, for our fetters were ordered only a fortnight later, and the delicate undergarments were soon languishing in our lingerie boxes, being incompatible with our now permanent fettered condition.

Not long after, as I have related, we were given the privilege of offering that service, that the too indiscreet widow had heretofore provided for Dr Boucher and Justice Rodsham.

In point of fact, the lady's defection worked to our advantage, for did we not now enjoy the inestimable boon of being guarded, guided and corrected by representatives of the church, medicine and the law? Until the advent of that worthy triumvirate, we had depended wholly on papa for our spiritual and mental health, and the discipline he deemed so essential, especially for the latter. His discipline invariably took the form of a greater or lesser application of the rod, but in future there were to be additions to the armoury of those who fought so valiantly to save us from the dragons of sin, lust and unwomanly forwardness.

This is not to say that papa's reliance on the rod had been ineffectual. Indeed, it had done much to keep us all in check. It was an experience that always gave us pause. When we were advised that we should report to papa's study and submit ourselves to the rod, I am ashamed to say that our feelings were too often not those of repentance and contrition that were mete for us at that time, but of stark fear, for that thick yellow cane cut right into one's soft buttock flesh, and hurt most excruciatingly.

The first bite was as of a bolt of flame searing the flesh. That was usually containable at first, but then a wave of pure agony would flood in, making one's whole body cringe, one's lungs burst to form the scream one's mind fought desperately to suppress.

And it never got easier to bear. One might have thought that, with time, one's sensitivity might be lessened. True, one's skin did seem to acquire a certain toughening, but this did us little good, since it only inspired papa to strike the harder or to increase our ration, until our bottoms showed the ruby, which he took to be the proof of a whipping well done.

This superficial toughening, however, made no difference to our sensitivity, and we seemed to have just as many nerve ends screaming their pain after each stroke, as the first time each of us had bared her buttocks for correction. We came to fear that aching length, and my belly would contract with terror each time papa withdrew it from its place of keeping, in his study cupboard.

It was not as if our new regime meant any diminution of the frequency or severity of our beating. On the contrary, with three males now available to share the duties, we tended to find ourselves called on to bare our buttocks, and mount the chair between our regular weekly visits for ordinary, and extraordinary, discipline.

But these interim whippings were not severe by our regular standards, seldom exceeding four or six strokes. The main innovation was the introduction of a monthly 'court' or accounting. Where papa had formerly merely referred to his book, in which he kept a memorandum of various faults he had observed, or we, in duty, had confessed and proceeded to execution without ceremony,

Justice Rodsham now sat at papa's desk, as if on his bench in the High Court, while papa played the role of prosecuting counsel, and the doctor gave them the benefit of his medical and scientific expertise.

Each of us in turn would step forward and stand with downcast eyes, though our high collars kept our chins from drooping, our hands clasped behind our backs, resting on our cringing buttocks, our stomach churning with fear at what might be to come. Our judge would make us answer to our name, then ask if there was any fault, not yet reported, that we wished to confess, warning us sternly, that pre-confession, or rather, the lack of it, would be taken into consideration when passing sentence.

'Under the law, any man is presumed to be innocent until found guilty, but it would be far too dangerous,' he declared, 'to extend the principle to the genus woman, and one should assume all such are guilty of something. It only remains to determine precisely what, before I deliver sentence.'

He would then call upon papa to read out the charges and punishments recorded in his book, since the last sitting of the court. When papa was done with the sorry litany of our failings, and the measures taken to improve them, we were again given an opportunity to make good any omissions in the list, before a general discussion took place among our guardians, as to our characters, our improvement or otherwise since it was last assessed, our sins and omissions, our habits and our deportment.

In fact, each of us was dissected like a beetle under a microscope, no facet of our lives being neglected, and each learned male contributing from his knowledge, observation and professional expertise to the assessment, and what means might be sought to improve us.

We would each wait in trepidation while our case was considered, for, though we knew that anything decided would be for our own good, we were sufficiently weak as to fear the inevitable searing of our flesh, it being certain that we would suffer some scalding of our buttocks, the only uncertainty being, to what degree, and with what supplements of correction.

We could be certain, too, that their exertions on our behalf, especially as they were obliged to spend several hours cooped up in our close vicinity, would aggravate the pernicious gatherings in their loins, and they would have to call upon our services to relieve the tumescence. Indeed, papa always took care that we came to the court, our forks freshly washed, our crotch chains dangling between our knees. Fortunately, our numbers exactly matched theirs, so none of us was obliged to offer her rear opening more than once in the evening.

Justice Rodsham, and the good doctor, went to great pains to devise additional disciplines that were exactly appropriate to specific sins and shortcoming, and we seldom left a 'court' without experiencing, or being promised, some new torment to curb our sorry natures.

For example, on more than one occasion it was remarked that Charlotte, although she never rebelled against, or even questioned directly, the stern regime under which we sought to become better women, she would give an opinion where none had been asked, or ask for information relative to our disciplines, beyond what was strictly necessary to understand how they might benefit us.

The tribunal discussed her case at some length on several occasions and, on the last, the judge, drawing on his immense knowledge of judicial punishments through the civilised world, recalled how, in the land of the Scots, such questioning had been curbed by the scold's bridle, or branks. The idea was taken up with enthusiasm, and the doctor made an immediate examination of Charlotte's mouth and teeth, prodding her tongue with his forefinger, while Justice Rodsham held her jaws open, as horse dealers do in the market. He took a number of measurements with his pocket rule, and undertook to obtain the necessary device by the next meeting.

We did not fully understand what a branks might be, nor its use, but it hung over us as a considerable menace for the next four weeks or so, since we had no shadow of doubt that we would not care for it. And although it was being primarily obtained for the better curbing of Charlotte's busy tongue, we had no hope that, once obtained, it would be reserved for her use only, and thought it certain that, whatever its woes, we would all know them shortly.

Nor were we mistaken.

Bridles & Other Curbs

We approached the next session of the 'court' with more than usual apprehension, and took care to be on our best behaviour, and to appear in the best state of dress we knew how, compatible with our status as sinners. Our hair was washed and carefully combed, braided tightly, and wound in neat crowns on our heads. Our accoutrements shone, the steel of our bands burnished, the leather at collar, knee, and waists, buffed up to a mellow gloss. Even the crotch chains, that chinked between our knees as they touched the links of our fetters, had been scoured clean. We were washed above and below, and our gowns were pressed and fresh.

We stood along the wall, facing the court, and waited, breathing lightly in our rib crushing stays, their laces tensioned up to harp string tautness. Our heads were held high by the tall and rigid collars under our chins, but we kept our eyes cast submissively towards the floor, so as not to challenge our guardians with our glances.

I hoped my knees would not tremble so much that the clinking of their chain would be remarked, and gritted my teeth, trying to still the flinching of my buttocks, and the sick feeling in my belly.

We had no idea what the branks might be like, but the pitiless cane was ever present and, apparently, inevitable. And that thought alone, of its deadly cuts in my tender flesh, the surging pain, the deep bruises that ached and throbbed for hours and were sore to sit on for days, was enough in itself to generate those expressions of the fear my body was filled with.

Marion was first to be called. She stepped forward to stand in front of the desk, and awaited the usual catechism. No, she had nothing to confess that our father had not already been made cognisant of.

'Do you submit yourself to your corrections, so as to receive their benefit to the full, making no attempt to mitigate their effects, before or after?' enquired the doctor, watching her closely.

'I do refuse any care that my sisters offer, if I feel that it is purely for the purpose of easing the helpful throbbing of my welts, but I have accepted certain creams that promote healing, even though they are also emollient and soothing. I feel that it is incumbent on me to maintain a healthy body, both to be ready for service and to avoid being a burden on others.' She appeared to hesitate at this point, and the doctor pressed her further.

'Yes, yes, girl. What is it?' he demanded.

'There is one other thing. After correction, my mind is usually in such a turmoil that I cannot sleep...'

'And for that you do what?'

She hung her head as far as her collar would allow.

'I caress that little bud that lies between my legs, until the tension bursts and I can sleep,' she said.

The doctor cast a look full of meaning at his fellow judges, but merely said that he had no more questions at that time. Papa and the judge exchanged significant looks, and the judge addressed Marion in his turn.

'Do you release your tensions in this fashion at other times, besides when you have been wrought by your correction?'

Again our elder sister hesitated, before replying in the affirmative.

'And how often do you perform this action, would you say?'

Another pause, then, 'Perhaps once or twice a week, sir,' was her reply.

The judge made a 'tsk, tsk' sound with his tongue, and said something I did not catch, to papa, who made an annotation in the leather-bound book, in which he kept our disciplinary record.

Marion was dismissed, and it was my turn to be called before the tribunal, they seemingly having taken a prior decision to call Charlotte last. Again I was asked if I had anything to add to my tally. I racked my brains, searching desperately to see that nothing was unconfessed, for the searing bite of that cane loomed nearer in my mind, and I would have spared myself any cut I could, coward that I was. But I could think of nothing, then, just as I was about to declare a clean slate, it came to me.

'If you please, sir,' I said, 'I too have been guilty of mitigating my corrections, by frotting my female bud so that I might sleep the quicker, once the tension had snapped within.'

The doctor pounced at once. 'Do you, too, resort to this frictioning at other times, and if so, how often?'

Much mortified, I kept my eyes fixed firmly on a small

69

ink spot on the carpet, in front of papa's desk, while I replied.

'Sometimes once or twice in a week,' I mumbled.

Again a whispered consultation, and another entry in papa's register. The whole proceeding had done nothing to quiet my apprehension, and I could feel my belly churning, while the points of my nipples hardened against the lining of my corset top.

When I was dismissed I stepped back to my place, and became aware that I had been sweating so much my gown was sticking to my shoulders, and I could feel the perspiration trickling down my armpits.

Now it was the turn of Charlotte. She was put to the same interrogation, and made similar replies. I had expected nothing less, since I knew that we all caressed our little buttons to ease ourselves, and had done since we first became women, and before. Most girls learnt the trick quite early, and get much comfort from it when troubled.

After her confessions had been duly noted between the covers of papa's leather-clad volume, they then turned to other topics.

The business outstanding from the last sitting of the court was the matter of Charlotte's poor control of her tongue, and the doctor's undertaking to secure a branks, or scold's bridle, which he now produced for the approval of the company. That is, the males present, the females naturally having no say in the matter.

I looked on, appalled, as he set it on the desk. The branks consisted of a cage of flat strips of iron, formed into an approximation of a woman's head, though somewhat larger, since it was designed to contain an actual female head within itself. The cage, for that is what it was, was split vertically at about the ears, and hinged, so that it could be put over the wearer's face and the rear swung closed and locked, to trap her within, with no possibility of removing it without the key.

A chain by which she could be led about depended from a ring over the nosepiece. Such a harsh and unyielding incarceration of the head would be punishment enough, discouraging idle chatter, but what made me catch my breath and my belly sink, was the cruel tab affixed to the inside of the cage where a tongue might be, but a tongue pointing inwards, not out. It was a flat piece of steel, fixed with thumbscrews on the outside, so that its exact position and angle could be adjusted to match the culprit locked within and, worse still, the underside of this iron tongue carried rows of short blunt spikes. Clearly it was intended to press down on the wearer's tongue and, not only enforce her silence, but rip her tongue should she nevertheless essay speech, merely gall her should she not attempt it.

I shuddered for my poor misguided sister, with her unruly tongue, but also for myself, for try as we might, papa still found reason to reprimand us for our remarks from time to time, and I doubted not that each of us would taste that hideous tongue before long.

For now, though, it was Charlotte who would have to wear that bitter bonnet, and the doctor came round the desk to fit his fearsome millinery over her delicate features. He ordered her to open her mouth, reinforcing his instruction with a prod of his finger, and lifted the front part of the open cage into place, the plate, with its horrible spikes, penetrating her soft mouth and bearing down on her small pink tongue. She kept her hands resolutely behind her back, as was the requirement, but her eyes bulged at the horror of what was happening to her, and she made nasal whines of protest as the rear of the cage was swung shut, forcing the iron tongue, and that of female flesh, into firm and painful contact.

The judge addressed Charlotte again.

'In order to assist you learn to curb your tongue, you will wear that bridle for the rest of the evening. One of you will come for the key when you are ready to retire.

'Meanwhile,' he went on, 'there is the matter of the solitary vice to which you are all prone…' It came to me that in confessing our usage, we had omitted to tell them that it was by no means always solitary. On the contrary, we more usually expressed our sisterly love for one another by bringing about those soothing and relaxing spasms one for the other. 'Such practices are not to be encouraged, and stripes will be added to your tally each time it is indulged. Three if confessed at once, four if it is only volunteered under questioning, and six full cuts if caught in *flagrante delicta*.'

More stripes! I cringed at the thought, and wondered if, in the comfort of my room and with my buttocks racked with pain from a whipping, my anus aching from rough distension, I might be tempted to take the relief there and then, and pay later with my hinds.

But the judge was not yet finished.

'Moreover,' he said, 'we deem it so necessary that you enjoy the full benefit of the lessons imprinted in your buttocks by the rod, that you must be denied the chance to exercise that soothing manualisation, and on such evenings you will keep your beds with your hands secured behind your backs, where they will be unable to reach those seats of Satan between your thighs.'

Oh! What doleful news. It needed no imagination to visualise the discomfort such bondage would cause us, but we tried to face it without showing our fear, for was it not all done with only our best interest at heart?

Now the judge was speaking again.

'Since each of you has only confessed to this sin under direct questioning, the law demands that you receive four strokes each.' He looked at papa.

'Undoubtedly,' agreed our mentor, 'I propose that each of us should deal with one miscreant, and afterwards, while she is suitably positioned, reduce that tension that I, for one, feel building so painfully in my loins. Do you, judge, take Marion, doctor you may judge best how Charlotte should be handled in the bridle, and I will attend to Annabel.'

And so it was done. Marion took her four strokes with her usual stoicism, and after, brought the judge off with her now expert sphincter muscle.

It was not possible to gauge properly how Charlotte reacted, since the sounds she made may have been on account of the interference with her normal breathing of the cage on her head, and the cruel blade pressing on her tongue. However, her whining and choking gasps did not indicate that she was insensible of the doctor's cuts to her buttocks, nor his ravaging of her fundament.

Finally I found myself mounted on that fearful chair, yet again. My nether cheeks cringed with a terror all their own, I could not control them. Though I knew I would only have to take four strokes, the long overture to this performance of the flogger's opera had sapped my courage, and I was as much undone by the four searing stripes papa laid on my bottom as by a full dozen on other occasions. I was much ashamed, and could only sob miserably as he reamed my anus, voiding his injurious juices in my bowel.

Our fetters replaced, Charlotte's bridle removed, we were dismissed to our beds, each carrying a pair of handcuffs. Poor Charlotte was in a sorry state. She had worn her hideous headgear for upwards of two hours, and her tongue was sore. She had no desire to make conversation, and communicated her needs as much as possible by means of signs, and nods of her head.

We tended each others hurts as best we might, though it goes without saying that we did not offer each other that comfort and relief that we had customarily shared.

When we had donned our night shifts we each retired to our own rooms and took to our beds, where we lay on our stomachs, as we would have done anyway given the state of our buttocks, and slipped the cuffs over our wrists, behind our backs, snapping shut the spring-loaded jaws. Now we could not give in to the temptation to touch those sweet sensitive buds between our thighs, but must lie and feel every throb of our stripes and twinge of our sphincters.

It was a restless night for each of us, and we were almost grateful to see the dawn and stumble to papa's room to have our hands released, that we might go to the stable yard and make our ablutions under the pump.

The bridle seemed to have a marked effect on Charlotte, and she was by no means as free with her tongue afterwards, even when no males were present and her remarks were addressed solely to us, her sisters, though it was not in her nature to not backslide occasionally.

I understood her caution better, when I had tasted the device myself. It was in the nature of things that our guardians would make each of us try the experience at least once, so that it might be a curb on our tongues should we be tempted to voice an unwomanly opinion or tone. In my case, I had merely explained how the wind was blowing from the east, always a difficulty in the vicarage, when papa had complained that I had made his fire to smoke and sting his eyes. For this I was sentenced to two hours in the branks, which I fetched immediately, and he forced the bit into my mouth, latching the rear of the cage behind my head to secure it.

It was a harrowing experience.

The steel plate pressed on my tongue, its stubby spikes not penetrating that organ, but causing me the greatest discomfort. My saliva gathered in my mouth, and I could not dispose of it properly by swallowing, and it dribbled humiliatingly down my chin. Try as I could, my tongue attempted of its own accord to shift the fluid to my gullet, and the action soon made it so sore that I could weep. Moreover, the weight of the cage rested on my neck or the top of my head, depending how I held myself. This was no hardship at first but, as time went by, it began to feel as if I carried a ton of weight, and my muscles screamed out for relief which did not come.

By the time I was released I had made up my mind to say no more than, 'Yes, sir,' and, 'No, sir,' in future, when speaking to my parent. At the time I would have been hard put to it to say even that, so sore and swollen was my poor tongue.

For purposes of education, and forewarning, even Marion had to wear the fiendish device, though one would scarcely credit that she would actually deserve it, so circumspect was she in her speech, so all of us soon knew the miseries of sore mouths and swollen tongues.

Nor were these the only sore and swollen parts of our anatomies. With the increasing frequency and regularity of our guardian's visits, and their apparently ever increasing sufferings from the female contagions that we were called upon to extract from their bodies, those muscle ringed orifices we gladly lent for the purpose were often as sore. For in their haste they did not always remember to lubricate those virile hoses through which they discharged the pernicious gatherings, and they were often quite rough with us, so desperate were they to get them out of their systems.

Marion seemed to fare worst. I think she was built a little smaller there than Charlotte or myself, and then again, she was perhaps, being older, not quite as elastic in that part. Be that as it may, for whatever reason she suffered from the frequent abrasion. When the gentlemen made to use her the discomfort caused her to whimper and twist her body, despite her best resolve to do her duty. This was a moment when we realised how blessed we were to have the services of the good doctor.

Marion was made to assume the usual position on the chair, as if to receive a flogging, but it was for inspection, not correction. The bent and spread position presented her anus admirably, and the doctor gave it his close attention, investigating with both finger and eyeglass. At length he came to a decision.

'It is as I thought,' he declared, 'acute haemorrhoids. I would suggest that we do not delay more than we have to. The sooner done the sooner mended, and her sphincter ready for use again.' He turned to his fellow guardians. 'Luckily I have bistoury and cautery in my bag. While we send for the instruments, perhaps you would help me secure the patient for the operation.'

There being no servants in the house of an evening, Charlotte was despatched to the stables to fetch the doctor's black bag from his trap. Meanwhile I was required to find straps, and strips of linen, to secure Marion to the chair. She was kept in her kneeling position, her thighs widely spread and her head down on the cushion. Her calves were bound tight to the chair arms, from behind her knee down to her ankle, making it impossible for her to twist her thighs or move her knees one inch on the armrests.

Then a long strap was passed over her back, under the armrests on either side, and back again to be buckled on her back and pulled up to the last possible notch, immobilising her still further by preventing her rising from her bent position. Finally her arms were pulled firmly round the back of the chair and her wrists lashed tightly together, completing her confinement and ensuring that she could not move any part of her body, the wide splayed thighs ensuring that her spread buttocks were held rigidly presented to the surgeon's work.

Poor Marion was much distressed by this painful surgery, but the doctor reassured us that it was a standard medical procedure, and in accordance with the best practice of modern times. He assured us she would make a good recovery, fit to take her place on the chair within a month or so, though she might have to endure considerable discomfort on the way to recovery, especially when attending to her natural functions.

As soon as we were permitted we removed the wrappings securing Marion so helplessly, and took her to her bed. But we could not stay long, for we had been strictly enjoined to return instanter to the study, to perform those remedial duties for our guardians, that their inflamed members demanded.

With Marion 'hors de combat', the burden fell more and more heavily on Charlotte and myself, until in time our poor sphincters started to show incipient signs of the same distressing symptoms that had led to Marion's need for surgical assistance. Our guardians viewed the possibility with some dismay, for how could they withstand the effects of the poisonous contagion if we were all three put out of action by the searing of our fundaments, and the need to let them heal before they could be safely used again?

The problem was solved by training us in a new and different way of drawing off the poison. We were introduced to the art of oral relief. We were shown how to take the inflamed and bloated organs into our mouths, stimulating discharge by running our tongues along the ridges on the stem, and around the edge of the satin smooth purple cap that formed its extremity, sucking lustily to engender the flow.

We soon became adept at this technique, and would bring our 'patient' to full flood in a matter of minutes. Then suck heartily until every last drop of matter had been drawn and swallowed, for the doctor assured us that, deleterious as it was to the male sex, it could do us no harm, since it was feminine engendered, much as a poisonous snake is impervious to its own venom.

With Marion able to play her full part in this new mode of keeping our benefactors in health, the burden was reduced until our sore rears subsided and could take up their duties again, for the gentlemen seemed to think the action of the sphincter more efficacious than that of the mouth and tongue. Though for myself, I could never understand why for their outpourings seemed total, and our suction ensured that not a drop was left within.

So now we had two skills, and just as well, for we were receiving a visit from one or both of our extra mural guardians nearly every night, and with papa's sensitivity to our malignant miasmas greater by the day, we were hard put to it.

With our new oral ability, Marion was able to share the

load with us from the start. But it was a month before she had healed enough behind to take her share of that mode, and even then the doctor advised caution so as not to risk a relapse.

You may imagine our nerves were constantly screwed to fever pitch by our frenetic activity, and we would have dearly liked to have sought relief through the peripheral stimulation of our pubic nerves, which the good doctor gives us to understand is the correct term for that process whereby we stroke our buds until the tensions of the day flood out of us, and leave us relaxed and ready for sleep. But this being now a matter for punishment, we have to make the judgement whether that solace is worth the price we must pay.

It always seems so, when we lie tossing in our beds, fretting with the undischarged excitement of the evening, our little fingers itching for our delicate buds, aching to rub in gentle circles until our bellies spasm and the ejected forces within us are made manifest as juices wetting our thighs. But when we are mounted on the chair, our buttocks screaming, as we would wish to scream but duty restrains us, we cringe at the thought of three more soul-twisting cuts, and regret dearly the fleeting pleasure we took. In any case, at the moments when we have most need of this relief, that is after correction, it is denied us by the manacles on our wrists, which prevent us from reaching between our thighs to perform the little miracle of healing.

With the so frequent visitors, the household had fallen into the way of dining together in the evening. Or rather, the gentlemen dined, and we women waited on them, preparing and serving their food, pouring their wine, and lighting their cigars after. In exchange for these small services we were rewarded by being fed portions from their plates, and allowed to drink from their glasses. We much enjoyed these generous expressions of their care for us, and tried to express our gratitude as well as we might, without appearing to be forward, or invite the infliction of the dreaded branks to curb our tongues.

It was their custom, while dining, to hold general conversation, the topic often turning to the vexed, and vexing, question of women, natural enough when one considered that, by profession, they were all responsible in their own way for trying to right the evils of this world, and where lay the source of most of those evils if not in women.

Naturally, they touched on the females of their own establishments, whereby we came to learn something of the nature and regimen of their households.

The doctor boasted a wife and three daughters, besides a quantity of female servants. His wife supported him in chastisement of the daughters, it goes without saying the maids were regularly whipped for their discipline as in any well-regulated household, but his spouse would not submit herself to his command or his rod. It would seem she must be a very unwomanly female, and we could quite understand how he might suffer so badly from the contagion that drove him to us for care, and felt even more obliged to help him in this matter, to atone in some small measure for those who we were ashamed to share the same sex with, so hateful did their behaviour seem to us.

Away from the baleful influence of his wife, the doctor, by reason of his profession, came into contact with many females in need of his expert help and guidance for their mental and physical health. Apparently he had many times advised husbands on the degree and mode of correction best suited to the disposition and physique of their spouses, and even demonstrated the same, for their better management. He also stated that he often recommended surgery for a variety of conditions, including hysteria, nymphomania and masturbation, though, listening at the table, naturally taking no part in the conversation, we women had no idea of what this entailed.

He also told of the County Asylum for Lunatics, to which he was consultant. A majority of the patients were of the weaker, female sex, so liable to disturbances of the brain, nature not having seen the need to overburden them in that direction, to compensate for the complication and general proneness to disorder of their other organs.

A great number of them had been consigned to the institution by their families on the grounds of moral turpitude, having been found in intercourse with men and, in some cases, actually bearing them children. When the babies had been born and put in the care of wet nurses, the young women were locked up, for their own good of course, and subjected to a strict regime designed to drive out the disorders that troubled them, and render their minds whole again through the disciplining of their bodies.

We recognised many of the elements readily enough, for they were the same that had had such a beneficial effect upon ourselves; cold baths, hard work, and physical restriction of the limbs, too much freedom of which invariably leads to loosening of manners and softening of moral fibre.

They were flogged regularly, too, but not across the buttocks, as we, but on the back. Like the loose creature we had seen at the cart's tail.

Justice Rodsham, apparently, was not so plagued by female company in his domestic arrangements, having no family of his own, with but a housekeeper to look after him and a parcel of maids. He did, however, come into frequent contact with females of all degree in his court, and when making prison visits. He gave many instances of the pernicious natures inherent in all us females, and our inclination to perfidy and moral turpitude. Amongst the more deplorable activities he had sought so hard to curb, was that well known weakness of our sex for letting our tongues run away with us. It seems that many are so lost to shame and decency as to berate their husbands and other men set in authority over them, such as fathers and brothers, not hesitating in some cases to pursue them in the streets to the public scandal.

He would usually suggest that the man should lay charges of committing a breach of the peace, since this charge could be tried in a higher court, where a wider range of more severe punishments was available. He was most impressed by the scold's bridle, as demonstrated on ourselves, and much regretted that it had gone out of use in England, though still retained by the sagacious Scots.

His preferred punishment in the majority of cases was a combination of the birch and hard labour. He would generally consult the husband as to how long he was prepared to do without the services of his recalcitrant spouse, some asking him to make the lesson short and sharp, others, usually with younger mistresses to serve their needs, suggesting that a prolonged incarceration was necessary to obtain significant improvement, without fear of backsliding.

The woman would be removed to the county gaol where, on reception, she would be stripped and shorn by the grim matrons who supervised the house of female correction. Once scrubbed with lye and hard bristle brush, she would be secured over a heavy block in the courtyard, her buttocks well spread by securing her feet some three feet apart, and drawing her hands down the far side of the block. In this position, with her belly and breasts pressed firmly against the rough wood, one of the most powerful among their number was employed to lash her bare and stretched hinds with a bundle of birch twigs, about three feet long and well pickled in brine. Such lithe limbs stung atrociously, scouring the skin.

The husband was generally invited to view this warm reception, and the judge often felt it his duty to attend. The number of strokes depended on the seriousness of the offence felt by the complainant, the length of the incarceration – the shorter the stay the greater the number to compensate – and the judge's estimation of the woman's potential for stirring up trouble. This same number of strokes would be repeated as a 'leaving present' when the sentence had been served, and the woman ready for return to her husband, or other male guardian.

During their stay in the house of correction, the women were worked hard for many hours each day, such labour being held to be excellent for their minds, as well as their bodies. The most usual form was the treadmill. This was a long slatted drum, some six feet in diameter. The women stood on the curved surface, gripping a horizontal pole set at the top of the slope. Their weight caused the drum to turn, and they were forced to keep continually walking up the steep slope for hour after hour, any falling back bringing a heavy strap about their sweating backs, their out-thrust buttocks or their straining thighs, as the wardress on duty thought most fitting and effective. It was hot, hard, unremitting labour and, since the perspiration ran from their bodies in rivulets, they performed it bare foot and naked, save for a scrap of cloth around their waists, no lower than their juts behind, for their buttocks must be available to the whip, dipping in front to just reach their mossy mounds, so that decency might be preserved.

The judge often felt it his duty to check that this aspect of the punishment was conducted with sufficient vigour, and would visit the gaol personally to inspect the women as they toiled. He was able to assure the company that where he visited there was no letting up, nor sparing of the rod. And as a consequence, very few women were ever known to re-offend, going quietly about their domestic duties, curbing their tongues, lowering their eyes in the presence of men, and generally behaving as is proper for womankind.

The doctor and papa joined with the learned judge in deploring the demise of the bridle in England, but enquired if all the traditional, and effective, means of regulating the conduct of unruly females had been totally lost.

'By no means,' he replied. 'I am aware of, and have given my encouragement to, many a village where the ducking stool is still standing, and a local magistrate willing to make use of it. 'Tis a most sovereign remedy for scolds. Likewise, there are still many whipping posts in use, where the scold, the slattern and the harlot may scream their repentance under the lash.

'I believe, also,' he went on, 'that there is one manor in the forest, where the Spanish horse is still employed. I have not seen it ridden, myself, but there is such an apparatus in the house of correction, where those who kick against the pricks may sit and contemplate the error of their ways. 'Tis said that even the fiercest termagant can be found bathed in tears and incapable of saying boo to a goose, after a night on the horse.'

The gentlemen were most excited by these revelations, and resolved to make trial of them as soon as maybe, agreeing amongst themselves that it would serve a very educational purpose if we were to accompany them on the expedition, a proposal that we received with mixed feelings. A ride in the country was always a treat, but we feared to see how the women might be suffering, and even more so, that our guardians might be taken by the idea that we might make personal trial of these punitory delights.

Since, however, it was not our place to query their designs, nor did they ever take into account the opinions of mere women, we held our peace.

Of Matters Medical

By now the evening was well advanced. The tales of feminine discipline and management had occupied the gentlemen through the soup, the fish, the mutton pie and the jam pudding, to say nothing of copious quantities of Claret and some Muscadet to accompany the desert. Now, with their cigars lit and the port to hand, they turned their attention to their charges – ourselves.

The doctor wished to take up again the subject of what he referred to as the pubic nerve. He made a further suggestion for the improvement of our health by the application of the best of modern scientific and medical discoveries, and the new theories of magnetism and the electric flux.

It seemed that after attending certain seminars at the Sorbonne in Paris, Dr Boucher had visited his colleague, and fellow worker in the field of female sexual disorders, Dr Dubois of that city. Dr Dubois was very eminent in the field. Indeed, he had probably done more to promote the benefits of the control and management of unruly and dangerous females, than any other, so our own worthy and trusted physician was always willing to give credence to his ideas.

Arising from the discussion on magnetism, and linking it to the current theories on the menace of 'active' sexuality in the human female, he had evolved the idea that the malignant emanations from the female, which so disturbed men and caused them so much distress, the higher functions of the male being disturbed by the lower functions of the female, these emanations he held, were magnetic, or perhaps, electrical in some sense, and might be contained by similar methods to those used by physicists working in the field today. His suggestion was that conductive rings, placed as near as possible to the prime sources of female energy, would trap the flux and neutralise it, so that the woman would cease to be a danger to the men that were exposed to her. Or at any rate, the danger might be mitigated.

We listened with interest, not knowing exactly what was planned. And eventually it was agreed to make trial of the devices.

A ring should be put in the hood of the clitoris, in such a way that it hung and encircled the trouble spot, and thereby contained the energy. Since the vagina was the next obvious site, communicating as it did directly with the womb, the introit of that passage should be closed by a ring through the labia minora, trapping any emanations taking that route. It was objected that this would hamper a bridegroom, but the doctor pointed out that upon marriage the one ring could be removed, and new rings put in the holes in each lip. The effect might not be so complete, but a young husband must expect to take some risks.

Finally they argued that the female principle also had its seat in the breasts. Rings for each nipple were prescribed, circling as much as possible of each teat and capturing those lines of magnetic flux that had their origin in the mammaries.

Since our breasts, as well as our lower bodies, were to be included in the experiment, we were for the first time to appear before our guardians fully in a state of nature. This was a cause of some embarrassment at first; papa had seen us after our morning dunkings at the pump, to be sure, but not the other gentlemen.

Our reservations were brushed aside, however, and additional stripes awarded for questioning our superiors' judgement, it being pointed out to us once again that our guardians were all professional men and, as such, above the usual restrictions of modesty. We felt very foolish at our ignorance, and humbly submitted ourselves to the biting rod in expiation.

The doctor in fact upbraided himself for being so neglectful as to omit our upper bodies from the periodic inspections he made of us, and took the opportunity to examine each pair of breasts thoroughly, checking them for size and weight, feeling their texture and testing the sensitivity of the nipples. How erectile, how easily stimulated, how closely connected to the lower organs, testing the connection by manipulating a teat with one hand while resting the other on our lower bellies, feeling for the first trembling of spasm, a fingertip within the furrow below waiting to feel the onset of lubricity.

When the good doctor was satisfied that he had the measure of our mammary physiology and response, we moved to the next stage.

Each in turn was made to stand, her hands behind her

neck, looking upward and thrusting her breasts steadily forward. The doctor took a strong needle, set in a wooden handle, and a piece of cork. Placing the cork against one side of a nipple, he selected the position for the entry hole on the other side, lining the needle up carefully so that the traverse might be true and level. When he was satisfied with the alignment he drove the needle through the teat, into the waiting cork, thrusting firmly through with a short unhurried motion. It hurt intensely, but even worse was the feeling as the flesh gave way before the rising pressure on the needle. For the nipple is a surprisingly tough and gristly organ, quite hard to penetrate from side to side, until the tissue gives way with an almost audible rupture, the sensation of which makes any woman's belly churn.

I said it hurt intensely, but only for an instant, though it took rather longer and dragged more whimpers and groans when the split gold rings were forced through the newly pierced flesh. Once done, however, there was but bearable pain. Much the same could be said of our rings in hood and vaginal opening. In some ways the piercing was easier for, though it pained us rather more, and each whined as the needle worked its way through the membranes, there was no comparable sensation of gristle bursting that had so affected us when the needle had transfixed our teats.

And now we had four gleaming gold rings apiece, one in each nipple, depending gracefully on our breasts, one above our bud, enclosing that member like an encircling halo, and the last astride our vaginal openings, like a guardian at the gate. I must admit that, as I regarded these elegant additions to my body, for so their permanence seemed to create them, my thoughts were less on their scientific and medical worth than on the beauty of their appearance.

And it seems the others were aware of similar sensations. Marion and I had long discussions on whether we were obliged to confess this secret vanity to papa and earn ourselves extra stripes. Eventually I agreed with her that, though it might be in strict terms, our duty, it would distract from the high scientific purpose for which the insertions had been made, and we should not disturb the gentlemen with such frivolous feminine matters.

Now that we had appeared before the gentlemen once in a state of full undress we found it easier to repeat, which was just as well, for amongst other ideas of the most up to date sort that the doctor had brought back from his studies in foreign parts, he now offered the suggestion that we would fare better if we were to let the air circulate on our skins as much as possible. Of course we already did so each morning in the stable yard, as we stripped to stand under the pump and, since the introduction of our fetters at the knee, we had worn no drawers, so some air could circulate around our lower bodies and between our thighs.

During the day, when women from the village were present and the groom was on the premises, anything more was not possible for reasons of modesty, but now we were enjoined, once the servants had left of an evening, to remove everything but our stays, stockings and shoes. And it was in this condition that we now waited on our guardians at their nightly dinners together, for most nights of the week we received at least one of our visiting benefactors.

Our breasts, resting on the half cups of our corsets, proudly displayed their rosy nipples, each teat bearing its golden ring. Our high collars, buffed until the dark leather glowed, held our heads proudly aloft, while the burnished chains at knee and crotch added their own sparkle to our appearance, the fetters regulating our gait to becoming femininity, and the crotch chains failing to hide two more gold rings, which, though covered were not concealed. Below the fetters our black silk hose was gartered at the knee, and on our feet we wore glossy leather boots; black, with heels quite three inches high, tight laced to halfway up our calves. The judge, a man of infallible taste in all matters pertaining to female dress and deportment, had chosen them for us himself, another in the multitudinous evidences of the care they took for us.

If you think we were guilty in some degree of feminine vanity, that awful vice that afflicts most members of our sex from time to time, you may be right, but remember, we paid fully for our vices, nor did we grudge the cost. Moreover, our guilt was mitigated if not quite extinguished, by the knowledge that we were kept so close controlled, and meticulously managed, that we posed no danger to the superior sex, unlike those women allowed to run free, their vanity a danger and a menace to all around them.

Excursion & Alarm

We were happy. We were protected and controlled, we were cared for and corrected, we were useful and busy. How could women in our position fail to be happy? Our guardians took every care for our wellbeing, mental and physical.

They regulated our lives for us, they ordered our dress, they gave us stern discipline, without which womankind runs amok to its own sorrow, and the destruction of God's superior creation, man.

They corrected us when we strayed from those strict limits of discipline, and controlled us with purple stripes. They kept us busy with household tasks so that we had no time to be bored and contemplate mischief, as women are ever prone to. They allowed us to wait on them at table, and shared their food with us, even letting us drink from their own glasses. And they gave us the joy of being allowed to serve them by drawing the poison from their bodies, that sometimes seemed to overwhelm them.

And do not think we were confined, or saw nothing of the world. Our guardians took us on many expeditions, some educational, some for pleasure, all enjoyable in some degree or other, and improving to our minds. On one occasion the judge came very early, we were still drying ourselves after our dawn rendezvous with the stable pump, to take the six of us in his carriage, to see the antique judicial punishments, still surviving in rural parts of the county, to which he had adumbrated after dinner that evening, some weeks before.

It was, indeed, a somewhat remote village to which we came first, one of those small communities dominated by the Great House, or Manor, and existing mainly to provide service to the gentry who were the proprietors of the land. It seems that the lord of this manor, a man of middle years and used to command, the district magistrate by virtue of his holdings had, but two months gone, taken to himself a bride from a wealthy London family. The lady, being town bred, or at least grown accustomed to the manners and ways of metropolitan society, was finding it difficult to adapt to the more autocratic ways of the country gentry with their womenfolk. In the city great respect was paid to women and their wishes; here the opposite held, and females were expected to show a proper deference to their menfolk. This was her first visit to her new husband's rural retreat, and she was still not come to terms with her status here. She had, apparently, already been warned that her behaviour lacked proper respect, and then she had overstepped the mark completely.

In these country areas, it was an accepted fact that the gentry might tumble the wenches of their households, and nothing thought of it. Milady, it seems, had refused to abide by the local ethos, and had not only upbraided her groom in front of the servants, when she had caught him with his britches down, pumping a rosy kitchen maid in the stables, but had, when he laughed off the matter, so far forgotten herself as to strike him with her crop.

Such an assault could not, of course, be overlooked, however new a bride she was, or high her station. Her fault was heinous and doublefold, for she had struck both a husband and a magistrate.

In the interests of good order in the district he resolved that no favour should be shown, and a public example made, to 'encourage' other females of all stations, by showing that not even the highest was exempt. In any case, it were kinder to check her early, lest she stray even further from the path of a proper wife and become a mere termagant, a misery to herself and all around her.

Accordingly we arrived on the village green, the dew still on the ground, to find a small crowd already gathered to see the lady whipped.

Under a spreading tree, in the middle of the green outside the church gate, there stood a tall stout post, adorned about its apex, some six feet from the ground, by a pair of iron manacles. To either side, at its foot, shorter posts, only half a foot high, were set in the ground, and each carried a large iron staple.

We had not been there above five minutes when the gates at the lodge opened and deployed a small procession, consisting of the squire, followed at a few paces by his lady, in turn followed by a frightened looking maid.

The squire walked purposefully, looking around to see who had come to witness his bride's correction. He was a large florid man, in his late fifties, powerfully built, and every inch the landed proprietor. His delinquent bride was a lady over twenty years his junior, of a very aristocratic appearance, tall, of a very fine figure, if a little on the slim side for rural tastes, who looked straight ahead of her, chin held high as if disdaining any who should see her shame. Her glorious dark hair was plaited into a great rope that hung below her shoulder blades. She was bare foot, and wore nothing but her shift.

I wondered, at first, that such a fiery and defiant creature should go so meekly to her flogging, but soon realised that, given the choice of walking freely to her doom, or being dragged kicking and screaming by the village constable, a lady of her breeding would chose the path that retained her some semblance of dignity.

Coming to the post, she looked to her husband in query. He nodded, and she slipped the straps of her shift from off her shoulders, letting it fall to her waist and baring herself from neck to navel. Her round and rosy breasts, still firm for all her thirty years, for she had not yet borne a child, sat proudly on her chest, their large teats puckered and hard, though whether from fear or the coldness of the day I could not tell. For whatever reason they stood out like small thumbs, still visible when she stood to the post, a breast on either side of it, as she lifted her arms to the manacles above her.

A rough looking man standing nearby, no doubt that same constable she had saved the duty of dragging her, advanced and secured the iron bands about her wrists, leaving her stretching up, her body pressed close to the wood, well worn at that point by the countless female forms that had sweated their agony and, it is to be hoped, their repentance, against it. She stretched even harder but a moment later, when the constable bent and pulled each slim bare ankle in turn to lash it to the rings on the side posts, thus spreading her widely and forcing her to go upon her toes.

The squire waved the thick black whip he carried at a thin bespectacled individual in the front of the crowd.

'Come, come, man,' he cried, 'are you to keep us waiting till past our breakfasts? Read out the charges, and madam's sentence, and let us get on with it.'

The clerk to the court drew out a paper and read.

'The Lady Camilla is found guilty of, firstly, striking a Justice of the Peace. Sentence, ten strokes of the whip on her bared back, to be delivered at the public whipping post. Secondly, of striking her lord and master, sentence, twenty strokes of the whip on her bared back, to be delivered at the public whipping post. God save the Queen.'

And the lady, thought I, for thirty strokes with that whip would make a breakfast difficult to swallow.

The squire spoke sharply to the timorous maid, who scuttled forward and lifted the great rope of hair from off the lady's back, draping it over her left shoulder to fall down over her breast. Now all was set, and the crowd fell silent out of respect for the whipper and the whipped.

Stepping to the left of the post, the squire measured his mark, then drew back his arm and brought the whip slicing down across the white back before him. It fell with a crack like a pistol shot, and the lady's head came back with a snap, but she made no sound whatever, though a livid red line sprang up across her shoulders, the end curling round her side.

Another stroke fell, an inch below the first, then another and another, and so on in dreadful progression, the lady jerking under the blows as far as her stretched position would allow, but making no more than anguished gasps at each cruel impact, letting out her breath again, hissing through her teeth.

After ten strokes she wore a ladder of slanting scarlet rungs from the top of her shoulders to her neat waist. Now her husband/executioner moved to her right side and repeated the ladder, delivering the blows from his backhand. If they were not as hard, I doubt the lady was aware just then, for she was beginning to show a little distress. Her gasps had become sharp groans, trailing off into a low moan.

By the time the second ten had formed another ladder, criss-crossing the first, her sounds were more urgent, though she still refused to cry out openly.

Her master gave her a short respite, then proceeded to the last ten, laying them on in two lots of five from either side, but this time he made them more horizontal and let the whip's end curl round her sides, to touch the delicate fullness of her breasts. She jerked with renewed vigour at this cruel assault on her tender dugs, giving a sharp cry at each and whining a little between, but it could not be said she broke, and she endured to the end without screaming or howling, though she was clearly hurt. Such fortitude is, of course, a mark of breeding, a case of *noblesse oblige*.

When it was done her back was laced and striated from shoulders to waist, the scarlet lines passing round her sides and onto the round white breasts. She stood at the post, her head dropped forward, her bruised shoulders heaving spasmodically. When she was let down she could, at first, scarcely stand, and threw her arms round the neck of the diminutive maid to support herself. But after a few minutes she recovered enough to stand upright and pull her shift up to cover her nakedness. Then, with her arm around the maid's shoulder for support, and leaning heavily on her servant, she made shift to walk back past the lodge, her back very stiff but her head held high.

The squire watched her go, then came to where we sat in the carriage still, from where we had watched her whipped.

'Morning, Rodsham,' said he. 'Doctor, your servant. These must be your daughters, Vicar. Won't you bring them in and take some breakfast with us? Warm work this early makes a man hungry. I dare say madam is a little warm too. But that's no reason she should not entertain guests. She shall be down directly, when she is decent dressed.'

And so we all followed him into the hall, and to the dining room, where the servants had already prepared a fine breakfast. Our guardians seated themselves and, habituated as we were to the practise, we made haste to get them bacon and kidneys, eggs and lamb chops, as they required, moving swiftly but demurely, then kneeling at their sides to be fed from their plates.

'Capital! Capital!' roared our host. 'Madam may show her repentance by the same service.' And he sent at once for her to join us.

In ten minutes or so she came down, dressed a little

informally, she could not have borne stays, but very composed, if a little pale. She moved very stiffly, which accorded with our own restricted movements and, obedient to her lord's command, waited on him just as we did on ours. Though she had been foolish, or worse, to have assaulted her lord so, I thought her very brave to have come downstairs and served him so humbly, not half an hour after she had been flogged. I think, though, she was much relieved when our guardians did not linger over their meal, but excused themselves, and us, saying we were due elsewhere shortly.

In fact, they were anxious not to miss the next on our itinerary. Duckings were, by tradition, carried out at noon of a Friday, and we had some miles to go. Thanking our generous host and his lady, we mounted again in Justice Rodsham's carriage, and bade the coachman make haste lest we be too late. We need not have worried, for he got us there and time to spare, and the gentlemen produced wine from a hamper while we waited.

It was a very pretty village, a ring of trees around a green, cottages on either side and, in its centre, a large and muddy pond, its surface coated with green slime, through which ducks drifted, dipping their heads to grub for worms in the murky depths. On the far side cattle came down to drink, adding their own wet brown contributions to the thick soup, the rapidly warming sun bringing out a thick pungent miasma.

On the side nearest to where we sat sharing the gentlemen's glasses, a long beam was pivoted on a block set in to the bank. One end of the beam carried a large stone, as a counterweight, while the other was adorned by a crude wooded seat; no more than a flat piece of timber fixed to the beam, with a narrow plank sticking up about three feet, making a crude backrest.

By now it was noon, and a noisy party came out of the inn, dragging between them a strapping young woman of, perhaps, twenty-five or six. A big girl, rosy cheeked, strong bodied and sharp tongued. She'd been tried by the villagers on the complaint of her husband, that she did nag him constantly about his drinking and had boxed his ears more than once, when he had come home from the alehouse with too much drink taken. Such behaviour could not be tolerated if the community were to live in harmony for, as more than one man pointed out, women had no voice in the proceedings naturally; if one wife were to practice such unnatural behaviour, would not they all, and where would they be then? Ruined, all of them, with no pleasure left in their lives, and only their wives' nagging tongues ringing in their ears.

So she was condemned to be ducked, and here she came, manhandled by two stout fellows who had their work cut out to manage her. I never saw a woman so unmindful of her duty to her man, and the custom of the district. They forced her, kicking and cursing, onto the seat, and tied her ankles together beneath the beam, her wrists behind the backrest. Now they swung the beam out over the fetid pond, her weight roughly balanced by the stone, so they handled it easily, just leaning on it to keep their end down, and her up. The aggrieved husband did the honours, crying out, 'Dunk her, lads. Dunk her once, and dunk her deep.'

With a great cheer they let go the beam, and the chair, woman and all, plunged into the murky water until she was covered quite in stinking green slime. The crowd cheered and counted, one and two and three, and the men threw their weight on the beam, dragging her out into the air. She coughed and spluttered, weed in her hair, her gown soaked and fouled, a fearful stink all around from the disturbed depths. As soon as she caught her breath she began to curse her husband anew, and every man in the village.

'Oh, ho,' said he, 'she still has fire. We must see if we cannot douse it quite. Dunk her twice, boys, and dunk her deep.'

Once more the men on the beam let go their end, and the cursing virago disappeared beneath the scummy surface with a great splash, disturbing the ducks, and the cattle in their muddy shallows on the other side of the pond.

Now the crowd chanted, altogether, one and two and three and four. This time, when they raised her, some of the spirit seemed to have gone out of her, and she spouted quantities of dirty water before she found her voice.

'You bastards,' she cried, her language a disgrace to the gentle sex. 'Call yourselves men, to treat a woman so? As for you, Tom Partridge, don't think I'll have you in my bed in a hurry. You've abused me enough. Get me down.'

'Not yet, lads,' he cried, 'she's still a mite too hot. Down for the third time, and let's see if that puts out the sparks. Dunk her thrice, boys, and dunk her double deep.'

This time, as she dropped into the green stench of the duck pond, the crowd chanted remorselessly on. One and two and three and four, five, six, seven, eight, nine and ten!!

As they hauled her up she fell forward in her watery seat, great gouts of liquid gushing from her throat. She gulped air, retching foul water, jerked in her bonds for above a minute before she could form words.

'Enough! Enough!' she cried. 'I'll be a good wife. You shall stay out as late as you will, only don't duck me again, Tom. I'll be drowned,' and much else, submissive and pleading, besides.

Satisfied at her repentance, and hopeful of her conversion, though knowing the wilful ways of women I would think him over hopeful, he signalled to his cronies to swing her in to land, where one released her bonds; no easy task, wet and slimy as they were. She fell at his feet, protesting her sorrow at having berated him so in the past, and swore to never vex him again. She made a sorry picture, kneeling in the muddy grass at the pond's edge, her gown soaked and ruined, weed in her hair, great streaks of slime and green scum on her face. Where was now the proud, defiant termagant, who had cursed him and his fellows but a few watery minutes before? Verily, the ducking stool had the most beneficial effect on even the strongest female, if applied with rigour.

Tom turned and led the way back to the alehouse, his manly honour satisfied, while she, her woman's place established, followed, dripping, at his heels, like a whipped spaniel. Our little party, edified and uplifted, left the scene to travel on to Sexton Hinds, where we were to visit the county House of Correction for Women, which lay just outside.

We arrived about the middle of the afternoon, and were met by the chief wardress herself, for Justice Rodsham was a man of consequence in the county, and to be treated with all deference. She was a veritable Amazon, a great strong woman, as tall as most men and built as broad. Her features, too, had more of a man's hardness in them than a woman's gentleness, and we women shuddered slightly at the looks she gave us, as if assessing us for punishment in her grim establishment. Still she treated us with civility, and invited us to take tea with her before touring the penitentiary.

It was served by one of the prisoners, a young woman showing signs of having been pretty before being brought here. But now dressed only in coarse brown gown, she was bare foot and appeared to wear nothing else, and kept her eyes fixed firmly on the floor, so we could see nothing of animation or character in her face. The wardress seemed to have instilled a very real fear in her charges, and we were soon to see evidence of her methods.

We asked our hostess what manner of offences had brought the women into her charge, and how long most would stay. She told us that most were there for offences against public morality; adultery, harlotry, defiance of their husband's or family authority, and similar heinous crimes in women. They had few felons as such, for thieves, murderers and infanticides, and the abortionists that aided them, either went to the gallows, or if they escaped the rope, were usually transported, formerly to the Americas, now to the new colonies in Australia.

After the tea, we followed her through the various parts of the prison. First the rows of cells where each inmate was locked up, when not working or undergoing punishment, in a stonewalled chamber, perhaps five feet by ten. Each contained nothing but a plank bed fixed to one wall, with neatly folded blanket, and a pail with wooden cover for natural functions. Light, such as it was, and air, came from a small barred opening high in the end wall. The door was massive, fitted with a heavy lock and a small barred opening through which the prisoner could be observed at any time.

Set apart from the main rows of cells, in a basement beneath, were a dozen more, thick walled and well separated, where prisoners might be kept in 'solitary', not only kept locked continuously, with no work or exercise periods, but not even able to hear the sounds of normal prison activity.

At the time of our visit there were five of these 'solitary' cells in use, mainly, we were told, containing women who had been judged to have shown too little respect in their altitude to the wardresses.

We went next to one of the workrooms, where twenty or thirty women sat at long tables, stitching more brown gowns, together with wardresses' uniforms and, we were surprised to observe, civilian clothing of all kinds. It seemed that the staff not only took care that their own wardrobes were kept stocked, but took on work for local merchants, that bought them little luxuries to soften the bleakness of their surroundings. Naturally these luxuries were not shared with the inmates, who had done the work that had earned them. These women were here to learn their duty, and expiate their misdemeanours, not to enjoy soft living.

In another part of the prison, we were shown a similar sized group at work in the laundry. Work was sent here by many local establishments; the hospital, the workhouse, etc., and also by the more worthy and wealthy householders. The women wrestled with blankets and sheets and all manner of dirty linen. They doused them in great vats of steaming water, rubbing them by hand on slatted washboards, wrung them out before taking them to the lines. Others sweated with flat irons, heated on an open hearth to produce immaculate creases and gleaming starched collars.

All these workers were watched closely by wardresses, mostly as large and as grim as their chief, who moved amongst them pointing out errors in their work, or reprimanding them for talking, reinforcing their strictures with blows of the long black straps they all carried at their belts.

We enquired where the remaining prisoners might be, for we had seen only about as many as would fill less than half of the long rows of cheerless cells, and were told that, apart from a number undergoing punishment, the rest were out on work gangs, and we would see them that evening when they returned.

Punishments were carried out either in the prison yard or the large square building next to it, set aside for the purpose. The yard held a whipping post and a block for birchings, where those women condemned by the magistrates, but spared the indignity of a public flogging, might be whipped away from the gaze of the crowd. At the time of our visit, however, there was no such sentence pending, much to the disappointment of our guardians, whose thirst for knowledge in these matters was unquenchable.

That is not to say that the yard was not busy. It was, in fact, a hive of activity. A number of women, of all ages and figures, marched round the perimeter, carrying on their backs large packs loaded with stones. We were told that these packs weighed from forty to sixty pounds, and were selected to be about one third of the bearer's own weight. They marched relentlessly on round the yard, lifting their knees high at every pace, their sweating bodies kept to their arduous and soul destroying task by slashes of the overseers' straps.

While the half dozen unhappy marchers kept on their inexorable round of the yard, two other offenders crossed it back and forth, back and forth, each carrying a heavy iron ball on each crossing, until they had built a pyramid of ten iron shot, each of about twelve pounds in weight. When each had built her pile, six in the bottom set, three above and the tenth on top, she had to dismantle it, one by one, running back to rebuild the pyramid on the other side of the yard. I do not know how many times each of them had completed this pointless and backbreaking exercise, but judging by their exhausted appearance, they had been straining under the heavy and unwieldy balls for some hours. And only the constant crack of the overseers' belts across their legs and backs kept them from collapse.

Nor were these the only defaulters. In the punishment room, off the yard, there were other devices for maintaining the strict discipline that was the reformatory process for these women who had failed to observe that docility and obedience so desirable in our sex for both our wellbeing, and that of the men we serve. We went inside and the first thing that struck our gaze was a great engine, or treadmill, that filled one wall. It was constructed like a mill wheel, a wooden drum about seven or eight feet in diameter, its surface made from a number of parallel narrow wooden planks, like the treads of a staircase wrapped around the circumference. A broad plank platform ran along its entire length, about three feet from the floor, that is, on the centreline of the machine, while a handrail was fitted above its centre. There was room for several women to work the mill at one time, and on the occasion of our visit there were four women, gripping the top rail, and almost running in their effort to keep up with the turning of the wheel. The effort of constantly climbing stairs, as it were, was obviously very great, for they sweated and heaved in their attempts to keep up, but it was not their labouring breath or grunts of effort that struck us into shocked gasps of our own, but their dress. The women were naked!

Each of them strained at her task as nature had made her. The sweat dripped from their bodies, running down the hot red marks of the straps that kept them moving, their muscles rippled and their breasts swung with their

108

efforts. I think our surprise must have shown on our faces, for the wardress made a point of explaining the reasons for the women's presence here, and their state of undress.

'That big slut on the end is here to cure her of laziness. She could well do as much work as a man, but she complains when sent on the work gang, and the overseers spend more time than she's worth trying to make her do her share. When she's spent a few days here she'll beg to go back on the gang. These two sorry creatures,' she pointed to a pair of under nourished young women tramping side by side, 'have spent too much time in the laundry, gossiping rather than working, although they know it's forbidden to speak in there.'

'And how long do they serve in here?' the doctor enquired, ever ready to accumulate knowledge.

'They work from seven to twelve, with but a ten minute break,' the wardress replied. 'At noon there is an hour when they may eat, and also do their share of prison cleaning, including their own cells. It would not do for them to feel that this substitutes for their duties; it is an additional punishment. In the afternoon they walk the mill from one till six, with a ten minute break again, mid-way.'

She gestured at the sweating crew. 'Since the punishment hall is by way of being a private place, and their efforts cause them to sweat like mares, we have them leave their prison gowns aside, rather than rot them with their sweat. Besides,' she added grimly, 'it leaves them bare to the straps, which can encourage them the more.'

'And will they finish tonight?' the judge asked in his turn.

'All but that slut on the end,' the wardress said. 'She'll come back on the morrow, and each day thereafter until she begs to go back on the gang, and we judge her ready to work her weight.'

'Why is the fourth here?' Charlotte asked, with her usual unfortunate forwardness.

The wardress gave her a look that seemed to suggest that she would enjoy the tutoring of such a minx but, aware of our prestigious guardians, kept her thoughts to herself and answered fairly instead.

We all craned to hear, for the young woman was interesting, indeed. About my own age, her nakedness revealing a very beautiful figure; curved exquisitely, though with no suggestion of plumpness at any point. Her hair was long and wild, dislodged no doubt by her exertions, very draggled now, but obviously cared for quite recently. She had a very beautiful face, firm round breasts, and long straight legs supporting full rounded haunches. Her whole appearance showed her to be a young woman of quality, despite the circumstances in which we found her.

'Ah, an interesting case,' the wardress answered. 'A very tasty piece, I grant you, but handsome is as handsome does. What you see before you is a bride that shirks her duty. She was wed a month since, but the marriage not consummated yet. She claims her young husband is either incapable or unwilling, for it was an arranged match as you would expect, both sides being gentry of the highest quality. But her mother-in-law has it that, in such cases, it is always the bride to blame. She has only to work hard enough at bringing her groom to the bed, all hot and hard, and nature will have its way. But this creature,' pointing at the panting girl on the mill, 'would not have it, and said she had done all she knew, and the fault lay in her son. Well, the noble lady was not having that, and took mistress pink cheeks here before the magistrate, who happened to be one of the family, and had her sent here for forty days for slandering her husband and wilful failure to consummate the marriage.'

'And what has she done to be put to the mill?' asked I, emboldened by curiosity and Charlotte's example.

'Why nothing, miss,' was the reply. 'Her mother-in-law declares she is a lazy slut, besides unruly, and asked that she be worked hard here, mentioning the mill herself. And since she is a good friend of the house,' I guessed that the noble lady had been generous to the head of the establishment, 'we were pleased to fall in with her wishes.'

Just then one of the overseers barked a command to the young woman we had been discussing, and she let herself fall back with the descending wheel, letting go of the rail and stepping off onto the platform, where she clung to the guard-rail, panting and trying to regain her breath.

'I thought you said they walked until six,' said the judge, 'and yet that young miscreant has been taken off with more than an hour to go.'

'Taken off the treadmill,' agreed the wardress, 'but she is not finished yet. She has been let down to receive her birthday present.'

'What! Presents in the prison?' roared his lordship. 'I thought this was a house of correction, not cosseting.'

'Why so it is, sir,' said the wardress hurriedly. 'Let me explain. Today the young woman is twenty years of age, and her mother-in-law sends her a special present. She is to receive one stroke of the cane across her naked buttocks for each of her years, twenty in all. Perhaps you would care to see it?'

Nothing could have been better calculated to restore the judge's good humour more effectively, for he was always eager to see justice done, and we all followed the wardress to the far side of the room, where the reluctant bride had preceded us. There we found her already 'horsed', her well formed body bent over a padded wooden horse, her feet parted a little to secure them to the legs at one end, her breasts lying on the leather top, her arms drawn down to secure them to the feet at the other end. Since the far end of the horse was significantly lower than the near, her hips and buttocks were thrown well up, her toes but barely touching the floor, and she was indeed very well spread for the rod. The chief wardress went to the head of the horse to address the pinioned rider.

'Well, miss,' she said, mockingly, 'such a thoughtful mother-in-law you have, to remember that today is your birthday, despite your slights of her. Since you are now twenty years of age, she has sent requesting that we give you twenty reminders of her regard, and so we shall, across these hinds, and with a penal cane.'

The young woman obviously lacked neither brains nor courage. Though she had only been in the prison for a few days, she had had the sense to realise that any show of spirit or resistance would only make her plight worse, and that she would do best to be obedient at all times, and speak only when addressed directly. Accordingly she held her peace, and the chief wardress signalled to one of the overseers, who stood nearby holding a wicked looking length of cane. It seemed to me much like that dire object with which papa, and our other guardians, struck so much fear in my belly, and fire in my buttocks. It was quite as long, thick and flexible, and I could feel my knees tremble and my belly gripe at the thought of it cutting into female flesh and, especially, mine.

Advancing to the bent buttocks on the horse, the overseer laid the rod across to measure her spot. I watched the taut rounds clench at the contact, as I knew my own did, rebelliously, despite my constant resolve to take my punishments wide open to the rod. I would suppose that this young woman, though my own age, had had less frequent acquaintance with such a rod. The overseer's arm drew back, raising the rod to shoulder height, gaining room for a full-blooded stroke, then brought it whistling down, cutting the air with a ripping sound before sinking into the soft white flesh with a sound like some monstrous twig snapping.

Dire Consequences

As the dire length of yellow rattan bit into the pale buttocks, with a sound that sent fearful spasms through my belly, and I am sure, through those of my sisters too, for we had heard it so often welting our own rounds, the young woman jerked in her bonds and gasped at the shock of the impact, then drew in her breath, hissing with the pain but bravely trying to endure it without crying out.

A short pause and again the cane sang as it flew down to cut the buttocks, a finger's width below the dark red line that had sprung up across their fullest part after the first stroke. Again the girl gasped and sucked her breath, but she hung on despite the pain that I knew, only too well, a rod such as this could raise in a woman's flesh. She endured a further four strokes with no more reaction, and the set of six blackening bars formed a broad band across her lower buttock, from its centre down to near her thigh tops.

The overseer handed the cane to another, who took it in her left hand, and stepped to the bending woman's right. Now the strokes were to come from the other side, and overlay the first set. The first of these new strokes seemed to take the victim by surprise. I think she may have been too taken up with her throbbing aching haunches to realise the change had taken place, or what it portended. Whatever the case, she squealed as the cane bit into her ripening welts, and moaned as the pain flooded back after the first shock. But she was a courageous young woman, and collected herself rapidly, adjusting to the new assault and taking the next stroke and the four that followed with only a little more sound than her first six.

Admittedly, a grunted 'ugh' accompanied each searing cut, but she held back from crying out openly, and only moaned a little between the strokes as she lay absorbing the pulsing agony that builds as the blood creeps back into the bruised flesh.

Now the first overseer took back the cane and stood to the left side. She directed her strokes rather lower than before, more or less on that slight fatty crease that divides the overhanging buttock flesh from a woman's thighs. It is, as I can testify from much experience of the same, a spot most sensitive to the rod, and seeming to burn in a manner less easy to bear than higher up the hinds. The unfortunate bride bent over the horse certainly found it so, for she gave a choked cry at each stroke, 'aaahing' and 'ooohing' in acknowledgement of the anguish she was suffering but, nevertheless, still maintaining something of her control.

She almost lost it when the second overseer took her from the right, overlapping the previous welts, but at least it did not come as a surprise this time. And although her cries at the impacts were urgent, still they might not be judged to be true screams, though she was sobbing now between.

When it was finished her buttocks was a mass of thick purple ropes, the twenty welts from her 'birthday present' difficult to distinguish.

She had shown amazing fortitude. Many times I'd had twenty and more strokes from papa or one of the guardians, but I doubt I could have sustained that score of searching cuts without conceding screams and shrieks of agony. Indeed, I felt quite sick thinking of it, and quite irrationally feared that I might be called upon to take her place; so much so that my knees trembled and my heart pounded in my breast.

As the reluctant bride was led away, her spine arched back in a bow of anguish, her bent legs hardly able to support her, her feet shuffling with her lameness as her bruised buttocks stiffened, I distracted myself from the nightmares in my mind of bending in her place, by turning my attention to the conversation between the chief wardress and the judge.

'A fine correction, well laid on,' said he. 'She'll be glad birthdays come but once a year.'

The wardress gave a smile that made me tremble anew at the horror of falling into her hands.

'Indeed, your lordship, *her* birthday has passed. But her new husband, whom she has treated so shamefully, will pass his twenty-second year next week and, just two days before her forty with us are up, her mother-in-law will be five and forty. I think she will remember *that* birthday.'

The afternoon had almost gone while we had watched the birthday celebrations, and it was time for the work parties to return. We watched from the wardress's office window on the first floor as they came in. The gates were opened to allow in a number of rough carts. In each sat a score of women, ten along each side, their right ankles fastened to a chain that ran down the bed of the wagon. As the gates were shut behind them and the carts halted in the yard, the chains were released, and the weary women stumbled out of the crude conveyances.

They were indescribably worn and dirty. Their short gowns, which were all they wore, were caked with mud and grime, and stuck to their bodies with their own sweat. Their hands were foul and worn also, their nails broken, their palms blistered, their feet cut and bleeding, for they had no shoes, though a few had found scraps of sacking in which to wrap themselves against the hardness of the road. For they had been on the road gangs.

The turnpike was crossing the county and the authorities had prudently helped to defray the cost of their keep in the penitentiary by hiring out the women to the contractors, to clear the path of the new road, to break stone for its bed, to dig cuttings and pile up embankments, to fetch and carry like beasts of burden, for it is well known that women are particularly well adapted, by their physiology, to carrying burdens.

I have never seen such worn and weary creatures, and applauded the good sense of those in charge for devising so effective a way of combining good husbandry with a regime that so obviously achieved its aim of introducing fallen women to honest toil.

When the last of the draggled and exhausted creatures had dragged herself off for the frugal evening fare, before 'lock up' for the night in their solitary cells, our guardians began to offer their thanks to the chief wardress and prepare for our departure.

'But will you not stay for the Spanish horse, sirs?' she asked. 'I think you will find it instructive.'

Nothing if not eager seekers after knowledge, our guardians at once asked her for details of this strange sounding beast, and she, anxious to please such worthy curiosities, set about an explanation.

It was, it seems, a form of punishment designed to 'break' even the most recalcitrant soul. It was generally reserved for those who fought the prison discipline, encouraging by their example lesser sinners who might otherwise have bent the knee and bowed the head before their keepers. There was just such a bad influence in the prison now; a widow of about seven and thirty, a fine strapping woman who had determined to carry on her late husband's trade of corn merchant in his place. The local growers and merchants viewed the development with some alarm. Not only was her unwomanly descent into trade in itself an affront, but she was also proving to be so astute that their own businesses were suffering. Their opportunity came when she was discovered entertaining the young women of the district to tea, and encouraging them to think of similarly going into lucrative trades, as she did. Worse still, it was reported that she had bolstered her case by remarking what dolts men were, and citing cases of business follies committed by their own fathers and brothers.

Such a thing could not be allowed, of course, for what would become of society if women were to put themselves forward as the equals of men. Such behaviour was flying in the face of nature and damaging to the fabric of society.

She was brought before a magistrate, who had little difficulty in being persuaded that her behaviour constituted corruption of minors and trying to take the girls out of the care and control of their fathers; how could any right thinking man conclude otherwise. At first it was suggested that, as no sane person could possibly argue that women were the equals of men, she should be committed to the local Bedlam for the insane, but wiser counsel prevailed. If judged insane her business would be run by trustees, and still carry her name. It was judged better to hold her responsible for her actions, so that she might be committed to hard labour in the women's house of correction for two years. And fined so heavily that she was ruined, thus proving that a woman was quite incompetent to run such a business, as it collapsed after only a year in her hands.

Though she should have learnt her lesson, and tried to redeem herself through meek and obedient service, she had continued to sow the evil seeds of her misguided philosophy among the vulnerable minds in the penitentiary. She had been flogged almost insensible twice, and still continued to drip her poison. Now the end of the road had been reached, and she was to be broken finally to the bridle of prison discipline. The doctor, always the technician, asked for an explanation of how this would be achieved, but the wardress was sparing of details, saying it could be appreciated best by viewing it in action.

Accordingly we delayed our departure, and followed the wardress back to the punishment hall. To a side we had overlooked before stood an innocuous looking device;

a simple structure of two sloping sides, constructed of narrow horizontal planks, each side about four feet long and a yard apart at the base, and leaning towards each other until they met at a point about four feet from the floor. The top planks met at a sharp edge, stained somewhat about halfway along, as were the sides below in a pattern like to a saddle. At the foot, on either side, were rings with long thin straps. The only other features of this innocent device were two vertical poles that were fastened to each end face of the apparatus, and projected about three feet above the top edge.

While we were puzzling over the manner of employment of the strange structure, two overseers arrived, marching between them the merchant woman so careless of her condition as to rate herself an equal of men and who, what is more, had attempted to disseminate her poisonous doctrine to innocent and impressionable females, seducing them from the proper duty they owed their fathers, brothers or husbands as may be.

As the wardress had said, she was a fine looking woman, the more pity she should have disgraced her sex so. She displayed a mature figure, though not fat by any means, with high rounded buttocks and firm breasts of an excellent shape, and tipped with large red teats, for as soon as she came to the Spanish horse she was ordered to remove her one garment, and stand naked before us. Although it seemed usual for women in the punishment hall to be deprived of their gowns, on the grounds that they were rendered more accessible for the overseers' straps, I believe that in this case it was done more to humble the haughty spirit.

First the woman's hands were bound behind her back, each wrist to just above the elbow of the other arm, and a collar, with two long cords depending from it, was fastened round her neck. During all these preparations the prisoner stood quite quietly, offering no word of protest, seemingly resigned to her fate though showing no sign of fear or repentance, looking in front of her with her head held high.

'That is a stiff neck,' observed the chief wardress, 'but I'll wager she'll bend it by morning.'

Now two stools were placed, one on either side of the horse, and the still proud prisoner invited to mount. With a look of disdain she stepped up onto the one, and swung her leg over the top of the horse, to rest on the other.

'Put your cunt to the rail,' ordered an overseer.

We recoiled somewhat at the coarse expression, but perhaps it was appropriate for such an evil sinner.

Once more she obeyed, bending her knees, until the sharp upper edge of the device was pressing at her entrance. As she came in contact, the overseer used her fingers to part the plump lips between her thighs, until they lay either side of the V that formed the top edge. Next they took the cords hanging from the collar, and attached them near the tops of the two posts at either end of the horse, leaving just a little slack, and went to stand either side of the horse.

At a nod from their superior, each pulled out one of the stools on which the woman stood, letting her weight fall fully on her crotch which, until then, had only partially supported her. She gasped as she felt the wood cut into her soft parts, but still made no protest. It seems she was fully aware of the futility of pleading or remonstrating with her correctors, since it would sway them not a jot, and she preferred to maintain her dignity in the face of adversity.

The overseers wound a strap round each shapely ankle, pulling them tight until her legs were stretched taut on either side, and adjusted the cords to her collar so that she could lean but little, forwards or back. The pull on her legs, and the cords to her collar, ensured that she could not cast herself sideways, and she must remain upright until she might be released, able only to adjust her position by but a small degree, and must needs sit on her tender female parts.

Watching her I became intensely aware of the chain that had been cutting into my own crotch since morning. But my female parts had only to endure the pull of the strap. Hers must carry her whole weight. I shuddered at what it might feel like to be seated thus, one's legs spread so that one's knees could get no grip to ease the load, able only to rock a trifle back and forth, making the choice between bruising the pubic bone in front, or the coccyx behind, the tender tissues between suffering whatever the choice.

One could see that the prisoner was already aware of the terrible situation she was in, for her body was tensed all over, the muscles in her thighs and back standing out like bunches of cord below her soft woman's skin. She constantly eased herself backwards and forwards, as far as she was allowed, obviously feeling acute discomfort already, and her night's vigil had scarce begun.

By now it was past seven o'clock, and all our party were in need of rest and refreshment.

'She's a hardened sinner,' said the wardress, 'and it will take a while to make her betray her feelings. Do you repair to the inn in the village, where you may find rooms for the night and a good supper, then return here about nine, or a half past? She should be beginning to sweat by then.'

Our guardians were pleased to act on this advice, and so were Marion, Charlotte and myself, for we had worn our 'uniforms' for over fourteen hours without respite now, and our necks ached, our knees were sore and the chains in our crotches seemed like knives.

At the inn we found that the landlord could offer us but one large chamber, with three beds in it, but it was too far to go back to the vicarage tonight, and papa took it, ordering supper the while which, when it came, proved to be very good. Our guardians seemed to have felt their day well spent, and showed their satisfaction by feeding us generously off their own plates, and giving us copious draughts from their glasses.

Thus it was in a much happier mood that we women set out for the prison, two hours or so later, for we knew we would very soon be able to remove our chains, and rest our weary bodies.

Not so the prisoner.

As the wardress led us into the punishment room, she turned her head to see who had entered, revealing a face drawn with strain, the mouth twisted as she fought to resist the pain gnawing in her vitals.

'This is an awful thing to do to one of our sex,' she groaned. 'As we are both women, let it finish now. I am being split in half.'

'You claim womanhood?' retorted the wardress. 'More like a hyena in a petticoat. Save that you have none, nor even a shift. No, mistress, sit there and be reminded of what you have between your legs, that says that nature has made you less than man. I'll wager, by morning, you'll have come to know the truth of it, and regret you ever preached such foul treason against your lords and masters.'

The woman gave a groan, and I would have been sorry for her, knowing only too well how cruelly such pressure in one's fork can serve one, but I remembered why she was here, and my pity vanished. What would become of the world if the natural rule of men over women were to be upset, and what unhappiness had she already brought on the young women whose minds she had poisoned?

The wardress wished us goodnight, and good rest, inviting us to come and see how well the reforming influence of the Spanish horse had acted when the termagant was taken down at seven, when her twelve hours were up. I shuddered to think of her there, all through the lonely hours of the night, perched on her agonising mount in the dark, unable to move, held secure, adding her own sweat of agony to the dark stains left by those who had ridden the terrible mount before her.

Back at the inn the gentlemen were eager for their beds, and we to ease ourselves of the chains that vexed us so sorely, so all were soon undressed, and in the case of the women, washed and soothed a little after the trials of our

124

long day.

However, our close proximity to the gentlemen, following a day that had seen them in our company continuously, not to speak of the many other women they had viewed in various states of undress, and distress, had so worked on our guardians that nothing would serve but that we should each bend over a bed, and do our duty by their bursting discharges.

This last duty performed, we were at last allowed to find our rest, each lying on a mat beside the bed of him she had just served; Marion, as befitted the senior, by Justice Rodsham, Charlotte with the doctor, and I, his favourite, by papa.

We all slept very well and were up betimes to go and see the Spanish horse relieved of its rider. Being from home, my sisters and I were unable to take our usual dip beneath a pump, and were allowed to use the gentlemen's hot water after they. I felt a little of conscience at the luxury of it, though it was but warm when it was my turn, but could not restrain the feeling of sweet comfort as I crouched over the basin to wash my still sore fork, before re-donning my chain. We took only a cup of chocolate, before the carriage came round to bear us off to the house of correction, where we arrived but a minute or so after seven.

'My apologies, ma'am,' said the judge, addressing the chief wardress. 'I hope we are not too late to see the outcome of last night's treatment.'

'Why think nothing of it,' the woman replied. 'We would have waited till noon for your lordship if necessary. The woman was not going anywhere,' she added in grim jest.

Once again we found ourselves in the punishment room, viewing the sorry figure on the horse.

There was nothing of pride or defiance now. Her head lolled as far as the collar would allow, her eyes were shut, her mouth open. She made long low sounds, like a mother crooning to her babe, but these were not the accents of maternal love, but of female anguish from a woman in extremity. She was still conscious and her lower body still rocked and writhed in a vain attempt to ease her pain, but she seemed quite unaware that there were others in the room, even when the overseers unfastened her legs and arms, unhooked the cords from her collar, and made ready to remove her from the sharp saddle she rode.

They lifted her, and she cried out as the wedge of wood left her flesh. When they set her on the floor she could not stand, but fell on her knees, then tumbled slowly onto her side, her body curled up into a ball, her hands thrust deep into her groin to clasp the bruised flesh between her legs.

'Now then, mistress,' the wardress addressed her, 'have you learnt your lesson, or would you ride further in search of enlightenment?'

'No more! No more!' she cried piteously. 'I'll not offend again. I'll submit me to men, as is right, but do not put me up again.'

'So you see the error of your ways, and your offences against man and God? Do you admit that men are your masters, and your duty to serve? Do you regret the bile you have fed your young acquaintance on, and that your

126

teachings flew in the face of nature?'

'Yes! Yes! I admit it all. I have been a disgrace to my sex and a corrupter of youth, but spare me the horse again.'

'I see you are cured of your madness,' the wardress observed. 'Take her away, and set her on the work gang.'

'Very efficacious,' remarked papa. 'The effect is quite wonderful to behold. A lamb that has strayed, found again. I must speak to the carpenter, whether he may construct such a device at the vicarage.'

If I had felt horror at the machine, just to see a woman broken on it so completely, how may I describe the terror that flowed through me as papa proposed one for our use. Surely we did not need to be broken so utterly? We were not perfect, perfection was reserved for the male sex, especially holy men and hermits, and mere women could not hope for it, as papa had so ably and persuasively proved in so many sermons. But we were docile and obedient, and surely our lapses from grace were adequately contained by the whippings we received, our sinful natures curbed by the constraints we wore.

I shook so much at what such a horse might be like, pressing with all the weight of one's own body on that delicate tissue between my thighs, that I had to brace my knees against their fetters to stop them trembling.

It was with thoughtful expressions and dark foreboding that we returned to the vicarage for, surely, we might expect to share many of the dire punishments, and disciplines, that we had witnessed women enduring this last twenty-four hours. Their cries and groans, their writhings and spasms, their choking sobs would soon be ours.

At first it seemed they would, and with but short delay, for papa commissioned Mr Bendham, the joiner in the village, to start work at once on his own design for a Spanish horse, and the two were soon in regular communication over its construction. Mr Bendham suggested many novel features, which our minds could not forebear to applaud, as shining examples of that technical genius that was transforming the manufactures of Great Britain, to the lasting benefit of its peoples. Though our bodies cringed from the implications for our suffering.

First he devised an ingenious system, whereby a plank on either side, about a foot from the floor, would swing out to form steps by which the horse might be mounted but which, at the pull of a lever, would drop down like the hangman's trap, to leave the rider mounted on the edge.

And what an edge!

Ever the craftsman, and determined to work with only the best of materials, he had suggested to papa that mere pine would not serve, and produced a piece of black yew wood, as hard as iron and shaped to a knife edge, that slotted into the top of the structure with all the delicacy of inlay on a Sheraton commode. His design also included a sliding yoke, which fastened round the neck and held the rider upright at all times, but gave no support in a vertical direction, thus eliminating any possibility of her taking any of her weight off the yew wedge splitting her crotch.

Though the shadow of this fearful device hung heavy over us, looming nearer with each visit Mr Bendham paid to the vicarage, other possibilities, favoured by our medical superintendent and our judge, were not so menacingly imminent, for both were from home.

The doctor had travelled to America with his friend and colleague, the celebrated Dr Isaac Brown, to spread their gospel of the management of women throughout the New World, that society there should enjoy the same benefits that had been so successfully propagated in Europe.

Justice Rodsham was also from home, having gone to sit on a committee considering whether corporal punishment for women should be disallowed by the courts. Needless to say, when the idea was first mooted, he conceived it his duty to go to London straightway, to put an end to such dangerous nonsense.

And now disaster struck, tearing apart our happy ordered world. One minute we were content, knowing our place, secure in the firm and wise governance of our guardians, sustained by our restraints. Without which, so papa, as a man of God, assured us, we would be as ravening wolves or scarlet women.

Papa's sense of duty was ever strong, and, in the absence of our other guardians, he conceived it his duty to take upon himself not only his share of the burden of controlling our unruly selves, but theirs as well. The burden was immense for, so it seemed, with the others away the danger of us erring was magnified in some way, such that he frequently found that each of us needed more than our usual weekly correction, and he would call us to his study at very short notice between our regular visits, to lay fresh stripes on wounds barely healed. Moreover, the effect of working on three of us without assistance meant that he was more and more infected by the female contagion, and required one or other of us to draw it from him every night.

One day, even this was not enough, and Charlotte was called directly from her dawn ablutions to quell the raging inflammation in him, after receiving six cuts of the rod for which apparently, she had become due.

That evening I went for my regular visit, my buttocks still sore and flaming from some dozen and a half of the cane they had sustained only two nights before. Now I was to receive another fifteen strokes, which reduced me to tears. While I stayed on the arms of the whipping chair he undid his britches, and entered me behind, a process less painful than of old, for the constant use had begun to stretch my sphincter somewhat, and I could receive papa's rock hard member with more ease than heretofore.

He set to work vigorously to work the poison from his system, and I to aid him by gripping him tight with my anal muscle and, it seemed, he came quickly to that climax that denotes the expulsion of the fluid, for I felt it hot and spurting in my bowel, thinking his gasps and snorting sounds much above what was usual, but supposing him just a little overwrought by the strain of controlling three young and vigorous women. As he gave his last choking gasp he fell on my back, but I thought nothing of it, for he often did, until he could recover his strength.

I lay there for one minute, two, not daring to move my position without permission, then imagine my horror as he slipped out of me with a small sucking sound as his member, still partly erect, left the tight sheath in which it

130

had been lying, and his body lurched sideways and fell to the floor.

I was torn between concern for my papa and my obligation to stay in my position until given word of release. Filial duty won; after all, I could always purge my disobedience by going back over the chair and taking my strokes again.

I knelt by papa, calling to him to reassure me he was in health. I felt desperately for a pulse, I leant my ear against his chest to listen for his heart, I laid my cheek against his lips to feel for his breath. Nothing! No pulse, no heartbeat, no respiration. Our papa had gone to his maker.

Dropping my skirts, which had stayed about my waist, I ran, unhampered by fetters, the loose band and the crotch chain rattling between my legs. I had not run freely so for months and the precipitate nature of my coming alerted my sisters to the presence of some catastrophe. They ran with me, as fast as their linked knees would allow, and came to where our dear papa lay. Nothing had changed, there was no mistake, no last minute reprieve.

He was dead.

After our first paroxysms of grief had subsided, we considered what best to do. We could not leave him there on the floor, his britches and his small clothes all undone. In life he had always maintained a rigid dignity, and we could not let it be less in death. Between us we carried him to his room and put him in a night-shirt, cleaning from his maleness that foul substance he had been expelling at his going, and the shameful excretions of my own body. We composed his hands above his prayer book, lying on his chest, and left him to his peace.

In the morning we found him thus, departed peacefully at his prayers, and sent for the attorney from Sexton Hinds, who was papa's man of affairs.

The funeral took place three days later. There was a large congregation of parishioners and admirers of the sermons that papa had published for the edification of men, lay and clerical, who had care of the souls and bodies of the weaker sex.

But of family there was none.

Papa had no relatives that we knew of. Certainly he had never spoken of any, and we had lost all contact with our mother's family after her death.

We entertained them all at the vicarage, and thanked those who had come from afar to honour a man of learning and erudition, whose teachings on the holy duty of women to submit to men, and of men to rule them with firmness and the rod, had been such a power for good in a world falling into the devil's clutches, for the evil one is well known to work his wickedness through the agency of women.

The surprise came at the end of the day when, all others having gone their ways, we sat down, wearily, with the little wizened attorney, to hear papa's will, and what estate we might have.

His will was simple.

He left everything he had to the three of us, jointly. He said he trusted that his efforts over the years had done much to curb the natural waywardness and destructive potential of our kind, but that we should be forever on our guard, and if we felt our natures to be taking control of our lives, to place ourselves immediately in the care of some strong man, who would direct us back to a proper path.

His trust in us was touching, but his estate took us quite aback.

We had known nothing of his affairs, thinking simply that his stipend had sustained us all, and would now cease, leaving us destitute once a new vicar was appointed to the living. So imagine our surprise to learn that he had left us a small fortune. Not the wealth of the truly rich, but enough invested in the funds to ensure we might live comfortably for the rest of our lives. Its origins were obscure, but it seemed in part to have been our mother's dowry, and part his earnings from the hundreds of improving works he had published.

We began to plan a glowing future. It was Charlotte who suggested that we should leave the county for Bath, that elegant and fashionable town, where we could live in ease and enjoy the arts, music and society it offered.

At first Marion demurred, saying that Bath was too dangerous for us; a city full of idleness, shallow girls and scheming matrons, and all manner of light people. But Charlotte persuaded her that we had all the more reason to go, since we might serve as beacons of light to those young women liable to be seduced by the licentiousness of the city, showing them how another way of life was possible, giving true fulfilment.

And so we began to lay our plans for the translation
from country vicarage to fashionable Bath.

The Die is Cast

The euphoria did not last. Although we still spoke of life in Bath, each of us was having private doubts, but did not, at first, share them with the others. By unspoken agreement we had conducted our lives, since papa's untimely demise, exactly as he had taught us. We still resorted to the stable yard at dawn, to squirm and shudder under the pump. We still walked with heads held high by our collars. We still wore our crotch chains, hauled up taut as bowstrings, though we did drop them at night to wash our sore flesh since, with no men to serve, they would otherwise have remained in place day in day out to the detriment of health and hygiene.

And at night we lay in our beds, wrestling with the temptation to ease our fretful spirits by stroking our pubic buds.

Now though, we had no one to confess these departures from discipline to, and fell into the way of going to papa's study, and entering them in his leather-bound ledger, just as he had been wont to do when we confessed our sins to him.

Could we continue this life in Bath, and if not, what would become of us without the support and discipline it rendered? We began to think more and more on how we would cope on our own, without a man's strong hand to rein in our natural female follies.

We would go to pieces.

We would go astray.

We would go, as papa never tired of warning us, to the devil.

Matters came to a head when Mr Bendham arrived one day with the finished 'horse'. We did not know what to do. We could not turn him away, and it was in any case a pet scheme of papa's, and must be honoured for his sake. So we had him take it up to the study.

After he had been paid and gone, we went back up to the study to view the new arrival. It was a fine piece of work, as one would expect from Mr Bendham, a craftsman of the old school. Its polished surfaces gleamed and shone. The brass work of the step mechanism winked in the lamplight, the black straps glowed darkly. Along its top the dark yew stretched like a strip of polished jet. We looked at it, and at each other. It was no surprise that Charlotte spoke first; she was still the forward one, but her words startled me, though they but echoed my own thoughts.

'Such an exquisite piece of work, and we shall never know its feel,' she said, almost wistfully.

None of us spoke for a minute, then Marion said, 'I wish to know what caused that poor deluded woman to recover her womanhood. With your help, I will mount the horse after supper, and make trial of its effect.'

We murmured our assent, and went down to prepare our evening meal.

Afterwards we gathered in papa's study and looked again at the seemingly harmless example of the joiner's careful work. Marion had us lift the plank steps until they locked in their raised position, ready to bear a rider's feet, then examined the yoke to support the neck, without taking any of the weight.

'I shall dispense with this,' she declared, and proceeded to take off her dress. Quickly she stripped to her stays, discarding gown and petticoats, boots and stockings, taking off her fetters, unlatching her crotch chain and tucking it into her corset lace, so that it was held well clear of her crease.

'Come, Charlotte,' she said, turning her back, 'make haste to secure my arms behind, as you saw that woman's,' and then, when Charlotte had carried out her wishes, she stepped onto one of the raised planks and swung one long leg over, to reach the other side. She stood a minute, her nether lips poised just above the iron-hard black rib of yew wood, lowering herself until she made an experimental contact, then spoke again.

'Annabel, dearest, part my lips there as you saw in the penitentiary, and Charlotte, do you fasten my ankles for me.'

The straps for securing the ankles were attached to the outer edges of the steps, so that when they fell to their lowered position, and locked in place, the ankles were drawn down with them, and the legs stretched taut. When I had gently parted her plump nether lips, she lowered herself fully, until the yew edge pressed firmly into her pink inner flesh, and sat with her weight mostly on that portion.

'Shall I lift the lever?' Charlotte asked, for the

mechanism that dropped the plank steps was operated by a lever at the end of the structure.

'No,' she replied through clenched teeth, 'it is not something I would ask either of you to do for me. Fasten a cord to it and put it in my fingers, then put out the lamp and leave me. Come back no sooner than a half-hour, to see how I fare. If you remain I might cry out for help before I have tasted it fully, or your tender hearts may mistakenly terminate my trial before it is complete.'

Charlotte and I looked at each other, doubtfully, but she was our older sister, and we had always deferred to her instruction. We made up the cord as she had asked, and left the room, taking the lamp with us.

Outside the door we both paused, with the same idea that we should stay a moment to guard against disaster, for neither Marion nor the apparatus had been tested before. We waited with bated breath for a count of ten or so, then heard a clack as the lever lifted and the steps dropped down and latched into place. Immediately there was a gasp from Marion, as of surprise at what she felt, then silence.

When the quiet had lasted a full minute, we crept away, reassured she was not immediately in distress, and feeling guilt at listening so furtively outside the closed door.

We waited below in some concern, watching the clock, and hurrying back up as soon as it showed thirty minutes had passed, taking the lamp with us. As we entered the room we were aware of a low groaning, and found Marion rocking slightly on her cruel perch, her body strained and tense. Though she was perhaps more softly covered than the woman we had seen at the prison, nevertheless her every muscle stood out below her skin, perspiration beaded her forehead, and tricked between her shoulders, her head lolled back as far as her tall collar would allow.

When she saw us she exclaimed in a strained voice, asking how long had elapsed and, when we told her we had come prompt at the half-hour, as she requested, she groaned again.

'Take me down,' she said, 'it feels as if I have been hung here more like three hundred minutes, not thirty. I have my answer now; this is a dreadful situation for a woman, and not to be endured. Quickly now, get me down.'

We hastened to do her bidding, undoing her wrists and releasing her ankles, then lifting her between us until she stood, or rather, half crouched, on the floor, for the pain in her fork led her to put her hands to it for comfort and hunch herself over them. We hurried her to her bed, and laid her gently in it, then soothed her to sleep without questioning her about the ordeal.

The next day comes Mr Attorney, with documents to sign, and the Bath papers, with details of the social whirl and, more to our purpose, properties to let. We had a busy day with him, and with the advertisements after he had taken his leave, laying them out on the table and trying to distinguish through the fog of fantasy what sort of dwellings they might be, for householders will ever laud their sheds as palaces, and their agents are even less to be relied upon.

I sensed that Marion's heart was not in it, and Charlotte,

too, seemed a little distrait, while I myself found my mind not as taken up by the plan for Bath as formerly, my thoughts returning to the previous evening and the scene in papa's study.

We made desultory revue of the houses on offer and then took our evening meal. After supper, Charlotte, who had been uncharacteristically silent, stood up and removed her clothes, leaving only her corset. She said not a word until she was stripped, nor did we question what she did.

When she had laid her fetters on the table she turned to us and said, 'I am going to the study. Will you come for me in forty minutes, to see how I do,' and left us staring after her.

I turned to Marion, but she nodded reassuringly and said, 'Let her be. This is something each must do for herself.'

In forty minutes we went up to the study, finding it in darkness. We could hear Charlotte breathing very hard and, when we had lit the lamp, discovered her, as we had known we would, mounted on the horse. She had been to papa's cabinet of curiosities and taken the handcuffs with spring catches, that he'd had off the Bow Street Runners when he had visited London last, and now they held her wrists securely locked behind her back. Before she had put them on, she had reached down each side to fasten the straps on her ankles. Holding the cord from the release lever between her teeth, she had set her parts to the wicked black edge of yew wood, then pulled on the cord to drop the side planks, so that they locked down, holding her legs straight and keeping her balanced on her fork.

Now she had been there near forty minutes, and like Marion, the strain showed. There were tears on her cheeks, and her muscles stood hard as ropes as she tried in vain to find some attitude less agonising than another.

'It is enough,' she gasped, as we came in sight. 'I know now what it means. Let me down quickly, I beg you.'

We needed no second asking, and in a trice had unfastened her legs and got her down. It took a minute to find how to unlock the restraints on her wrists, but then she clasped her centre, as Marion the night before, and curled herself around her pain until it eased enough for her to straighten, and thank us for rescuing her.

The next day we carried on our self imposed regime, still true to papa's memory, but we were all very withdrawn. I can only guess at the thoughts that troubled my dear sisters, but I know that my own were partly on what our future might hold, but mainly on what they had experienced and I had not.

That evening, after supper, I rose from table with no more word than Charlotte before me, and stripped down to my stays and collar. At the door I turned to them and said, 'Come for me in an hour.'

They nodded in understanding, and I climbed the stairs to the study.

By the light of a candle I found the handcuffs, set the steps, arranged the cord from the lever where it was in reach. I mounted the device, throwing a leg over the apex until I was standing upright on the two steps, and leant over sideways. I found I could just reach sufficiently to set the loop of the strap about my ankle, and draw the buckle tight. When I had secured the other, I leant forward as far as I could and blew out the candle, leaving myself in inky darkness. Now I drew my nether lips apart with trembling fingers, and set myself gently down on the hard sharp edge. As my weight began to bear on my tender tissues between my thighs, I began to get a first faint inkling of what might be in store, but I pushed on with my design.

I had purposed to explore what manner of torment this might be, just as Marion and Charlotte had done already, and I would not turn back now. I took the cord between my teeth and put my wrists into the cuffs, snapping shut the half rings, so that they would not open again. Now I was totally secured, and could not leave until someone released me. Now there only remained that last, crucial act that would plunge me, without reprieve, into that pit of anguish I had seen the others writhing in before me. I settled my fork as firmly as I might upon the painful ridge, my toes only taking a little of my weight, and made to pull the cord.

But my coward body rebelled, and would not do its duty, fearful of what it might mean. My brave sisters had been weeping after little more than half an hour, and the mature and masterful woman in the prison had been reduced to a whimpering wretch, all her boldness fled. I was determined that I would make trial for myself of this breaker of woman's mutinous spirit, and resolved that I would release the lever on the count of five. Slowly I counted them out, focusing my thoughts entirely on the fact that, on the count of five, my head would go forward and the lever would

142

move, blotting out the consequences, and thinking only of the need for the action itself.

The stratagem worked.

Blindly, unthinkingly, I counted off the numbers and on five, just as I had willed it, my head bent forward, taking the cord with it. The lever moved, the steps fell away from beneath my toes, and my legs straightened, letting my whole weight sink onto my most intimate and delicate female parts.

Dear God, how it hurt from the first! I gasped as the full pressure bit into me for the first time. It cut into my pubic bone in front, for I was still leaning forward, even though the cord had dropped from my mouth as I had opened it in shock. I rocked back to ease it, and the blade of the horse cut into me behind. I tried to find a point between, but only served to cut more deeply into my softest tissues as well. There was no position where one could escape, or even mitigate the grinding ache below. I found my body tensing, the muscles hardening as I had seen them in others. I sat rigid for a few moments, until the pain went beyond endurance, but then moved slightly, relieving the first hurt a trifle but merely transferring it to another portion of my tender anatomy, where it built up from the merely excruciating to the unbearably dreadful. And I would move a fraction again, in a vain attempt to find some surcease of the agony.

I sat there in the darkness, concentrating on my hurts. There was nothing to distract me, perhaps nothing could, and I began to see how a woman put in this position would look inwards to her soul, and see and repent her wrongdoing. From time to time I heard a strange moaning sound and did not realise for a long while that the weird keening came from my own lips. Tears ran down my cheeks, and every now and again my careful equilibrium was shaken by a belly-deep sob, which rocked me on my knife-edge, sending a new peak of savage pain into my vitals.

My hour on that dreadful mount, for Marion assured me they had come on the very tick of sixty minutes, was the longest of my life, and seemed like a dozen years of torture. When they found me I was moaning and sobbing, almost unable to speak, just croaking, 'Get me down, for pity's sake, get me down.'

They hastened to comply and I lay on the floor, curled into a ball, holding the bruised flesh between my legs with both hands, as if I could somehow pluck out the throbbing agony that still raged there as the blood was restored to the tissues.

When I could at last contain the ache I tried to stand, but had to be assisted, for my legs had become weak as jelly. And when I essayed a step, the pain broke out anew and I had to shuffle with my legs splayed wide, resting on my sisters' shoulders, as they helped me to my bed.

The next day Marion, our leader as always, sat us at the table when our frugal breakfast was done, and broached the subject that had been overshadowing us for days.

'We must give some thought to this proposal to remove to Bath,' she opened. 'It is a sinful city and full of snares and traps for weak women who can be seduced into luxury, and ease, forgetting their duty to the senior sex, and the pleasures of service, in the vice of being served.' She looked from one of us to the other.

'Tell me that I am not deceived in thinking that both of you have found doubts in your deepest minds as to the wisdom of the undertaking.'

We both admitted it was so, and she continued.

'I think we are particularly vulnerable. Papa made it abundantly clear that we were weak creatures, and in need of a discipline and a restraint much above the commonality of womankind, and we have become used to this support for our frailness. How do you think we would fare if we were to lose it?'

'I think it would go ill with us,' I replied, and Charlotte agreed.

'I was the instigator of the plan,' she confessed, 'and still I hanker for it at times, but, more and more, I know in my heart that we need a man's strong rule. Oh! Bath would be delightful, I know it, but would we be happy without our fetters? Without the sharp sting of correction when our guilty selves tell us we deserve it? What would stop us becoming a danger, to ourselves and to every male we come in contact with, if we are not subjected to another's will and rod?'

My heart almost burst to hear my own fears and doubts, that I had hugged to myself these last ten days, expressed so lucidly by another, and know that I was not alone in looking with apprehension on our coming change of life.

'But what can we do?' I wailed, quite in despair, now

that my fears had become expressed, rather than suppressed. 'Dear papa is gone, and we are alone.'

Marion put an arm round me to comfort me.

'Hush, Annabel,' she said softly. 'All is not lost. We have no commitment to Bath, and will make none.'

'But we cannot stay here for ever,' Charlotte objected. 'There will be a new vicar appointed to the living soon, and we shall have to leave the only home we have ever known and, even if we could stay, how would that serve our needs?'

'I have an idea,' Marion replied. 'Listen and I will lay it before you. We must turn to our other guardians. The doctor will not return from the Americas for some months yet and, in any case, his household is already overstocked with women.' And such women, I thought, recalling the grim mother and the stony faced daughter, a young woman as devoid of pity and human feeling as a stoat among rabbits. 'But the worthy judge has but a housekeeper, and a large house, with rooms for all. We would not come without dowries; our inheritance gives us the means to pay our way, in addition to the service we would take pride and pleasure in giving. He should be returning from the commission at any day. Is it your will that I should write to him, appraising him of our situation, and begging him to take us in and keep our weak womanly spirits in decent bondage, and disciplined restraint?'

We fell on her neck, drowning her with our kisses, thanking her for her brilliant scheme for our future.

The letter was written that night, we all colluding in its composition, ensuring that it conveyed the true depth of the submission we offered, and the strong hand we craved, and despatched to the judge's house, the other side of Sexton Hinds, the very next morning.

Within four and twenty hours we had our answer, and we burst into tears of happiness as Marion read it to us, her voice trembling so, she could hardly continue.

It seemed that Justice Rodsham had returned from his labours on the commission on judicial punishment, where he had partially succeeded in stemming the treacherous tide of misguided philanthropy that would remove the reins of corporal punishment from females, with all that that implied for the wellbeing of society, to find a parlous situation in his own household. As stated before, his only servant living in the house permanently, was a housekeeper, a fine looking woman of close on forty years, but buxom and well built, with fine features, long black hair, rounded bosom and buttocks, that had been with him since she was a young woman in her twenties. It seems that the creature had betrayed him by letting herself be got with child. Whose we could not tell, for it seems she went out but little. Knowing that her condition could not be hid much longer, she had confessed all immediately on the judge's return. There was no chance of her being allowed to stay on, the scandal would be too great, and she was to be despatched to distant relatives in the West Country, where she might disguise her sins under the cloak of being recently widowed, and bearing a posthumous child.

Meanwhile the judge was without a housekeeper, and we might come and take on that role. Weeping anew at his generous spirit, we hastened to compose our acceptance, and soon we were seated in the carriage he sent for us, on our way to our new home, and the comforting arms of discipline and correction so necessary to the female good.

We took little with us, save our small valises containing what clothes we had. We wore our fetters, our chains, our collars, as we hoped we would for ever, and I cradled in my arms that fat leather-bound journal in which papa kept the record of our transgressions and corrections.

The trap and its pony were given to George, the groom, as a gratuity, while such of the furniture left in the vicarage that the new incumbent did not wish to purchase for his own use, was to be sold, and the proceeds divided amongst the daily women who came in to share the housework, on condition that they renew their vows to love, honour and, especially, to obey their husbands, else it was to be taken from them and sent to the women's house of correction, for the use of its stern governess.

All else we had brought away followed in the carrier's cart; papa's cabinet of curiosities, with its whips, canes, straps, chains and restraints. That dread armchair on which we were used to pay for our sins with the stripes and sufferings of our buttocks. And the Spanish horse, that worthy mount that can carry even the most recalcitrant of females on the painful journey back from sin to salvation.

Once they, and we, were safely installed in the judge's unyielding care, we were sure our happiness and health would be assured.

Plus a Change

We arrived at the judge's home in the late afternoon, with barely time to put our modest belongings in the rooms set allocated to us, and see that the carter carried the 'horse', and papa's cabinet and armchair into the judge's own study, before we must set to, to put the house straight for his comfort and prepare him a meal.

Subsequently we were sent for to that same study, where he read us a stern lecture on the danger in which we had stood, having acted with independence of men for many months, and decreed that we should start our rehabilitation, and show a proper submission to the master of the house, by submitting to a flogging that very night, tired and weary though we were from the journey, and the trauma of being uprooted from our home of so many years.

'It is best you start in the manner in which you intend to continue,' he assured us. 'A little fatigue will only make you more receptive to the rod, and its curative powers.

'But first,' he added, 'there are some small formalities to conclude, regarding your income. You will have no need for funds of your own, since you will be living under my roof, and I will make you such allowances as are necessary from time to tine, for household expenses and any strictly necessary items of feminine expenditure as may arise, judging each application on its merits. You will, therefore, each sign a note to the manager of our local bank, authorising him to pay over to me such dividends and other income as it accrues.'

We could find no argument with this reasonable request, although we had made shift to run the old home for some months without male aid, and we each signed a note as indicated, trusting to the learned judge to correctly evaluate the validity of our requests for personal funds, should the need arise. Often a man will see clearly that what a woman thinks is necessary for her appearance or hygiene is, in fact, nothing more than vanity or extravagance.

The business concluded without delay, we turned our attention to that so familiar armchair, in its new and unfamiliar surroundings. In fact, the difference was not so great. The judge's sanctum was much like that dark austere chamber that had been poor dear papa's place of work and study. A largish room with heavy desk, bookcases and leather furniture of suitable sombreness, and decorated in an appropriately dark and brooding fashion, that was nicely calculated to banish all levity from one's thoughts on entering, if indeed there had been the slightest lightness of disposition among any of us when summoned to that place of judgement and execution.

It was not so crowded that it could not receive the familiar chair, the awesome Spanish horse, and the cabinet, with its cargo of corrective instruments, and still leave room for full free play of those same rods and straps.

It was quite like old times as, one by one, we bared our lower persons, mounted the chair, our knees widespread by the spacing of the arms on which we knelt, and lowered our heads to present our buttocks fully to the judge and the formidable rod he had selected. It was one of the more difficult canes papa had purchased for our maintenance, and I found myself weeping tears of shame for my fear and humiliation when having to spread my buttocks on the chair and, especially, at the feeling of openness behind, where my rather plump and pouting pudenda showed boldly between my parted thighs.

It was too long since I had been made to abase myself in this manner, and it showed. I was blubbering freely before even a stroke had fallen, and writhed and sobbed under the rod as, three months before, I never would have done.

By the third stroke I positively howled. My hips weaved, seemingly of their own volition. I could not control them, and the fourth also heard me giving tongue, as that brutal cane fell across my unpractised buttock, the welts now thick and dark on the previously pristine surface. It crossed my mind, even in that extremity, that they would probably never be wholly without mark again for the indefinite future.

But the thought did not persist long, driven out by the fifth cut, a beastly stroke, somewhat lower than the rest, indeed, on the gluteal fold itself, such a sensitive spot, even when used to correction of this strength, unbearable when so ill-prepared. Once more I howled and the rod returned, to sear me not a finger's breadth below. In the position we adopted on the well spaced arms of that dire chair, one was peculiarly vulnerable to a stroke like that, on the thigh more than on the buttock, and it could be excruciating. Could be and was on that occasion. I writhed and sobbed without restraint.

When I had quietened somewhat, rather than giving the order to dismiss and dismount from the chair, the judge addressed me on the inadequacy of my performance, and the need for me to do better. As an aid to this rehabilitation, I was awarded two extra strokes, and promised I would have the six to do over again if these were not taken with sufficient stoicism. You may be sure I made neither sound nor movement under the rod for those testing extras. The fear of having to take more of the same was even greater than my distress at the pain of the present visitations to my poor sore buttocks.

Though I hated them at the time, when I was able to contemplate my aching buttocks objectively, in the privacy of my bed, it was some small comfort to know that I had made amends by taking them with better dignity. I had not been called upon to relieve the judge's evil humours, since only one sphincter sufficed, and Marion did the honours, as befitted the eldest girl.

We had cast ourselves upon the judge's charity. I mean, in the sense of caring for our moral needs, our financial requirements were more than satisfied by our father's legacy, at a time when the doctor was abroad, spreading the gospel of his surgical treatments for feminine ills and, by the time he returned, we were safely installed in the judge's home, and settling down to our duties there, benefiting from regular and unremitting discipline, that kept us healthy in body and mind.

He did not delay to visit his old friend, the judge, and with great generosity, undertook to be our medical superintendent, as in the days when we lived in papa's vicarage, and he had been a frequent visitor.

Indeed, on the occasion of his first visit to our new home, we were made to submit to a full examination, to see how our bodies had fared in the intervening months.

'The female body is a complex mechanism,' he warned us. 'Liable to quickly lose its tune if not properly exercised, and prone to develop strange maladies if not kept under a strict regimen.'

We were instructed to strip ourselves entirely, not even retaining the corsets and restraints we seldom otherwise were without. We stood in a line, arms at our sides, chins up, but eyes cast down so as not to seem to be challenging our male superiors.

When the doctor had given us an overall viewing, he called on each in turn to get up on the heavy desk and lie back while he probed further. When my turn came, I found the hardness and cold of the polished wood strangely disturbing and, again, I had got out of the way of allowing my body to be handled freely without shrinking. It was further proof, if any were indeed needed, of the frailty of women, and how far they will backslide if the reins are loosened even for a moment. It only reinforced the wisdom of our mentors in putting us back as quickly, and as strictly, as possible, into that moral corset and stern rule in which we had flourished before.

The doctor's probing was searching. First he greased his hand, and introduced two fingers into my vagina, stretching, though not rupturing, the hymen and seeking out the inner lining and the soft nose of my cervix, where the neck of the womb intrudes on the vaginal tube. He explored thoroughly, until I began to squirm at the discomfort and prolonged tension induced by his manipulation.

He cautioned me to stillness, but withdrew and examined the bud of my sexual nerve, then bade me turn onto my belly and draw up my knees under me in a frog-like crouch.

The pose served to throw up my buttocks, and I was even more exposed when he made me part my knees widely, opening up the divide and letting the cool air play on the pouting button of my anus. For since resuming our service of the gentlemen's juices, I had found my nether orifice to have once more become slightly inflamed, being conscious of it at many times during the day, even when not serving in the study, and always when answering a call of nature.

While I had been adjusting my position, he had freshly greased his hand and I soon felt two fingers probing the rose of my sphincter. They burrowed deep and were joined by a third, and then a fourth. By now I was breathing hard, being hard put to it to maintain my pose without flinching, so great was the pressure. He withdrew a fraction, though his fingers never wholly left their lodging in my anus and, when they returned, they had been joined by a thumb. His whole hand formed a wedge, which he drove with unrelenting pressure into my poor sore anal ring.

At first he could only make but little headway, though what he gained pained me deeply. He growled at me to loosen up and let him enter, reinforcing his demands with several violent slaps of his hard hand on my bare buttock. I concentrated all I could, remembering the advice we had been given once, that a gesture as if trying to expel some sordid solid from one's bowel in fact opened up the sphincter, allowing entrance of a male member or similar. It worked in this case also, though the doctor's fist was not to be compared with a mere penis, and stretched me horribly.

Nevertheless, with a great effort on his part and many groans on mine, the greased palm entered until the sphincter closed about the wrist, still painfully distended, but less excruciatingly than when the widest part of his hand was passing through the narrow opening of my anus.

The sensation was unbelievable, unbearable, totally overwhelming. I gasped and groaned, writhed on his impaling arm like an eel on a fork, uttering small sharp cries in a jagged stream of sound.

At last he ceased his internal examination and withdrew. His exit was much faster than his entrance, and the sudden extraction of his hand, besides the inevitable stretching of my sphincter again as the widest part passed through, seemed to act as a suction pump, feeling as if my guts had been sucked out behind it. I lay puffing and blowing on the desktop for a minute or more, before I could regain enough strength to descend and start to put my dress in order once more.

And my sisters had not fared any better. Where Marion had been spared quite such as intrusive an examination of her rectum, she had been obliged to submit to such a forceful stretching of her nether lips that tears had come to her eyes, while Charlotte had not only endured an internal examination almost as brutal as my own, but had had her nipples seized in forceps, and drawn out until she bit her lip and moaned at the pain. It seemed a severe way to treat tender female flesh, but doubtless the doctor understood best what must be done.

As a result of these medical explorations, we were prescribed a number of treatments over and above our regular regime. In my own case, these consisted of a series of hot oil enemas, taken twice a week, each of two quarts, hot enough to almost scald, and held for fifteen minutes before relief was allowed, on pain of unspecified but fearful penalty if released sooner.

Marion was made to stand, legs widely spaced, for thirty minutes at a time, with small vices clamped to her nether lips, from each of which depended two one pound weights. The ordeal was aggravated by her being made to stand totally still, any movement causing the weights to swing and clash, whereupon the time endured to date was ignored and the thirty minutes calculated from the new starting point. She seldom got free in less than an hour, and shrieked when, at last, the clamps were withdrawn from her cringing flesh.

Charlotte was subjected to a similar ordeal, but in her case a weight of two pounds was attached to each nipple. At least she did not have to maintain stillness to avoid clashing, since her breasts were widely separated, but she nevertheless held herself mighty stiff to mitigate the action on her stretched breasts and teats.

It was ten weeks before the doctor decided that his treatments had done their work, and that we might drop them from our routine; the physical deterioration subsequent on our temporary deprivation of male authority, dispersed by medicine as effectively as our mental degeneration had been repaired by strict correction at the judge's hand.

At about that time, too, we had acquired a third guardian. During papa's lifetime, we had had the benefit of the three principal pillars of society; religion, medicine and the law. The last two we continued to enjoy, but there was a vacancy for a religious mentor.

But not for long.

The judge was acquainted with a churchman, a bishop no less, who had lately returned from the Far East, and been appointed suffragan to our local diocese. He was invited to dine at the judge's home, and after our very first meeting, undertook to see to the health of our souls, as the doctor and judge took care of our bodies and conduct.

We had only been told that we might expect a guest for dinner, and you may imagine our astonishment, mixed with hope and dread, to find a tall austere figure, dressed in black apron and gaiters, the only relief in his costume the white tabs at his neck, a purple sash about his waist, and the gleaming jet of rows of tight buttons that ran down his form-fitting gaiters from thigh to ankle, outlining muscular calves that spoke of a strong body beneath his other regalia of office.

After dinner the judge announced that he would conduct

his usual inquisition into our state of moral health, and need for further discipline, and invited the bishop to delay his departure in order to witness how well we were cared for. Accordingly, we were subjected to our normal catechism followed by penal correction on our cringing buttocks, which we bared in the usual way despite the presence of this senior churchman. We hoped our naked femaleness would not offend him, but I fear he was struck down by that same affliction that so troubled our guardians on these occasions, his body filled with malignant juices, the pressure of which had to be relieved if he was to remain hale.

As usual I was the last in line to be judged and corrected and it was, therefore, my freshly corrected buttocks, with their fifteen stinging welts, that he seized in his steel-like grip, as he presented the episcopal prong to my tight anal ring. He was indeed a mighty man before the Lord, as the Good Book has it, and his massive member drew a groan from my bitten lips as he forced himself into me. Several painful minutes later I had progressed to loud strangled grunts with every stroke he made, but consoled myself for my pain with the thought, as he gave half-a-dozen last rapid drives and I felt his juices explode in my belly, that I had performed a necessary service for the Anglican church, a rite to whose urgency the bishop's vigorous behaviour was ample testimony.

When he had recovered his breath, and adjusted his bishop's apron to cover his loins again, he pronounced himself much taken with the principles already established for our care; that women, being weak, needed to be constantly restrained, and that suffering was a sure way to salvation, or at least, an aid to avoiding damnation.

He had spent some time in Imperial China, and offered to instruct our guardians in alternative methods of female control to those already practised, so that comparison might be made of their efficacy. While we were, naturally, flattered and grateful for his interest, I for one could not suppress a chilling shudder in my belly at the thought of more, and greater, ordeals to come. I strove to control my weakness and express proper thanks for what we might be about to receive.

These gifts of care were not long in materialising. The bishop had acquired many mementoes of his years in China, especially it seemed, of those instruments used in the imperial harem for the better regulation of females, a subject on which he seemed to have made himself somewhat of an expert. He had expressed a desire to meet us again as soon as may be, and a few days later returned to dine with us again.

This time he did not come empty handed. After dinner he produced a curious device which, he assured us, was called in China, where it had originated, a *kang*. It was a circular piece of wood, or rather made up from several pieces of timber fastened together. It was a form of wooden wheel, some three feet or more across and over two inches thick, made from teak or other dense hardwood, and very heavy.

The disc was split along a diameter, with a hinge at one end and a hasp at the other. In the centre was a circular cut-out, of a size to fit a female neck and, on either side, nearer the rim, two further, smaller openings suitable for a woman's slim wrists. He proceeded to demonstrate on Marion. As eldest she found it her privilege to pioneer nearly all the various means our guardians took such trouble to provide for our better regulation.

With her neck carefully positioned in the centre hole, and her wrists in the flanking pair, the device was closed and a padlock slipped into the hasp, making it impossible to remove without the appropriate key. Now she had lost the use of her hands entirely, and it did not take us long to begin to appreciate the true horror of the position. Fixed thus, a woman could not fend for herself in any way. She could not feed herself, nor even brush a fly from her face, nor spilt food from her chin, since her hands could not reach in that far. The width of the wheel meant that she could not pick up objects, even from a table, nor do anything to repair her toilet.

Moreover, she would be entirely dependent on others for those natural functions that must inevitably arise during any prolonged incarceration in the *kang*. Either she must humiliate herself by asking another to hold up her skirts while she squatted to pass water or relieve her bowels, or she must foul herself as she stood. In either case, she could not clean herself after, and must ask another to wipe her between her legs, or in her cleft.

Sleep was not easy, though one learnt to lie on one's back with the edge of the wheel wedged into the angle between head board and mattress, though the position was precarious and any movement in one's sleep was liable to have one rolling sideways and waking in terror and discomfort.

Just to wear the hideous device for any length of time was torture, one's neck and arms beginning to ache after only a few minutes, to burn after half an hour, to scream in agony after half a day. We each of us were sentenced to periods in the *kang* from time to time, sometimes even to days at a stretch, and we rightly came to fear it greatly. I for one never quite overcame the shame and humiliation of having to ask another woman, or perhaps especially my own sister, to lift my skirts for me to relieve myself, since she must necessarily stay holding my clothing while water gushed from my slit or, horrors, while I strained to empty my bowel as quickly as I might, to shorten the ignominious performance. Sometimes even this was not possible, for my inhibitions froze my bowels, even though but minutes before, I had abandoned my vain efforts to keep their exigencies in check, and begged my sister to aid me.

And then, ultimate shame, to have to bend or squat, opening one's thighs while someone else plied wet cloth between one's nether cheeks, washing away the traces of one's degradation from one's fundament. Or employed a drier portion of material to wipe the last warm golden drops where they dripped from between the plump lips of one's sex. I often came nearer to tears from these degrading acts than from the most aching cuts in my behind from whip or cane. The shaming of it was bad enough, the helplessness of the position added to it tenfold, and we all feared it greatly.

It had fallen to my lot, in a wholly natural manner, to

service the bishop, just as I had serviced that other man of the cloth, dear papa. Since, as I have already remarked, the right reverend gentleman was possessed of a more than usually adequate manhood, the act was painful for me, a matter of no consequence of course, I being only a female. But much more importantly, difficult for the bishop to inaugurate, although once entered, he made good shift to ram me thoroughly to his complete satisfaction.

He opined that, while a tight ride was a blessing, we might all suffer some easement of our fundaments without sacrificing our efficacy as extractors of their harmful effusions. Having obtained our other guardians' agreement, he undertook to provide the means for this easement for, he assured us, the problem was not unknown in the imperial palace, and methods had been devised there to cure the condition.

Accordingly, some three days later, for the bishop had formed the habit of calling at least twice a week to see to the care of our souls, we found ourselves required to prepare a buffet meal, that could be set out beforehand, and to come to table, ourselves, devoid of gowns and petticoats, wearing only our stays and gartered stockings. In a mixture of curiosity and trepidation, for a novel summons always heralded some new pain or humiliation for us, we complied, though woman-like, our curiosity ensured that quite apart from the obedience we owed, we would never think of balking at the call to duty.

We found that, besides the sideboard full of cold meats, bread fruit and wine that we had set out previously, the dining room now contained a stout wooden bench, quite wide and long enough for three to sit on, with space to spare between.

And these spaces were well defined for us. Set into the bench were three cones of dull bronze, perhaps an inch across at the tip, which was adorned with a ball of the same diameter and swelling at the base to at least two and one half times that dimension. The cones stood about eight inches high and were formed, at their base, into a wide flange which appeared to be attached to the bench by screws, thus ensuring it and the very solid timber frame were effectively one piece. In contrast to the ancient oriental aura of the standing bronzes, this underpinning of plain stout timber was obviously from the shop of some local joinery.

We were instructed to line up with our backs to the bench, and the meaning of the order did not allow for much doubt as to the next proceeding. Marion appealed on behalf of us all.

'Sirs,' she pleaded. 'If we are to be stretched, these unfeeling stumps of bronze may tear the linings our tender rear tubes, unused as they have been for three days now. May we not at least use a little of the butter set for your repast, to ease their entry, and thus spare us actual injury? I do not believe it will interfere with the expansionist capabilities of the treatment.'

It was fairly said, and the gentlemen listened to her prayer with care. After consulting the doctor, the judge gave his permission, and we each took a little of the fresh farm butter, set out on a silver shell, and applied it to our threatened anuses, which had been cringing at the thought of penetration by the monstrous phalluses that menaced us.

Now we resumed our places, and the bishop gave the order we had been expecting, and dreading.

'Set your fundaments against the stretchers,' he commanded, 'and let your weight come on them, until they sink into your bellies.'

Lubricated as we were, the first part was comparatively easy and cost us but little pain, the smooth balls sinking in under our weight with little difficulty. As we sank though, so the discomfort grew. Not only were we painfully stretched by the increasing girth of the pillars of bronze, but they seemed to fill our bellies, causing us to breathe with more and more difficulty. We still wore our steel-bone corsets, that constricted our ribs. Now, with our belies filled with cold metal, even our diaphragms were impeded, and our shallow breath came in short rapid pants as we sat with heads thrown back, and open mouths.

If we had thought our position unbearable we soon had cause to think of it, in retrospect, as the very pinnacle of comfort. Each of us in turn was made to lift up her knees. A length of broomstick was passed under them and we were made to pass our forearms under the stick and clasp our hands around our lower legs, where they were seized and secured together with thongs. Now every ounce of our weight was on our bottoms, and our high drawn knees ensured the cones were forced to their utmost depth into our protesting bowels. We groaned collectively as we tried to adjust ourselves to this ultimate penetration, not believing that there could be worse to come.

'Although they are well stretched,' the bishop was saying, 'the effect can be even more pronounced, and accomplished quicker, if the woman can be induced to move about a little, to work the wedge in her bottom, altering the angle at which the stressed sphincter lies, and moulding it into shape.'

Dear God, I thought, I could no more move than fly. Even now the strain is killing me, and even the slightest movement would be excruciating.

As if he could read my thoughts, the bishop continued his homily.

'Unfortunately, it is sometimes difficult to convince the woman that she should make the effort. They seem stubbornly reluctant to obey properly given instructions in the matter, while so impaled, on what the Chinese describe so picturesquely as the "Enhancer of Perfumed Fundaments", and it is usually necessary to provide some additional encouragement.'

I shivered at what this might imply, then froze again, even the mere trembling that had shaken me arousing fresh degrees of discomfort in my poor stretched bottom.

The bishop came forward but, with my head back and my eyes half closed as I concentrated on my private pain and breathless apprehension, I could not well tell what he did. There was some movement below the bench, a flare, as of a match being struck, I could smell the sulphur, and then silence for a while.

Slowly I became aware that the cold shank of metal in my anal opening was warming. Some of the chill had gone out of it already, from contact with the wet inner warmth of my body, but now I was convinced it was actually more than just matching my own body heat, but beginning to exceed it.

Within a minute I was sure of it – the bronze wedge was definitely getting hotter!

Another two minutes and the heat was beginning to get uncomfortable, and still it increased. And in another minute I could stand it no longer, despite the anguish I knew I would cause myself, and I wriggled on my perch to try and move the heat to another part of my tender ring. Judging by the groans on either side of me my sisters were also experiencing the same effect, and were equally helpless to escape the inevitable consequences.

'You see,' remarked the bishop, a note of smugness in his voice, 'nothing elaborate. A simple candle set below the bench, and heating the bronze though a prepared hole. They cannot resist its influence, and I'll warrant we'll see them dance a merry jig before we're done taking our repast.'

And so we did, and sang them a mournful song to go with it; moans and groans and piteous cries of, 'For pity's sake, sir, remove the heat. It is burning up my belly. I shall be ruined for all time,' and much else besides from each of us, for the pain in our tender passages was unendurable.

And the gentlemen took no notice of us.

'Rest easy, gentlemen,' the bishop reassured them. 'The candle is nicely calculated to scorch them without burning. True, they will be a little discommoded for a few days, when passing their motions, but there will be no permanent harm done, and see how vigorously they work their tight rear tubes against the expanders. An hour a night will quite suffice to ease them, and we may enjoy the first benefits at once.'

And so they did, immediately they had finished their brandy and cigars, pushing the debris of their meal aside for us to clear when we had recovered sufficiently to resume our duties. In the meantime those duties were to consist of offering our tortured anuses for their use.

But first they must be extricated from the appalling spires on which they were impaled. It was not as easy as it was to set them on those hideous pricks, for we had near lost the use of our arms and legs, even when they were released from the thong and poles that had held them rigid and useless for so long.

At first we could do no more than try and stretch them, moaning afresh as setting our feet on the floor altered the angle of our bodies to the invasive cones and awoke new torments in our bottoms. But gradually we eased enough that we could raise ourselves slowly off those brutal bronzes and, with our guardians' help, stand swaying weakly.

But not for long.

We had only been released so that we might serve, otherwise we might well have been left even longer for the better reconstruction of our fundaments. So now we must turn and kneel over the same bench we had just quitted, a hot stem of metal, sticky with our own juices, resurgent between each pair of us.

I could have well done without this further reaming of

my poor bumhole but, compared with the dreadful invasion I had just suffered, even the bishop's mighty manhood seemed comparatively mild and, at least, soon withdrawn, leaving only a slight additional soreness, and a sticky ooze, behind.

The gentlemen then bade us goodnight, and retired to their rooms, leaving us to clear away the dishes and make good the house, before making our usual preparations for the night. I reflected, as I secured my 'saddle strap' between my legs, reawakening the soreness in my ravaged behind, that at least we had been spared the disciplinary accounting, and searing cuts of rod or cane that followed, that were normally the culmination of these bi-weekly dinners.

Besides the kang, and the enhancer of perfumed fundaments, the bishop had other souvenirs of his oriental ministry. We endured in turn 'The Butterfly's Kiss', a small jewelled clip, whose extravagant name describes its shape but does not convey its effect, for it is applied to the bud of the sexual nerve, and is anything but a kiss. The serpent's bite would be more appropriate, and we each mewled and writhed as we stood, hands behind head, trying to absorb its terrible hurt, to demonstrate that fortitude it was designed to test.

There were 'The Milk Needles', so named from the milky pearls with which they were decorated, and the teats into which they were plunged. And the 'Celestial Sandals', celestial in that only a goddess without weight could bear them, a flesh and blood woman hobbling and moaning from the devilish little points set in the toes and heel. We whined and writhed too, when anointed with the 'Passion Honey', a sticky substance exactly matching the sweetness for which it was named, but compounded from radish, peppers and exotic Chinese herbs, it's viscous nature causing it to cling to the tenderest of feminine tissues, and its burning bite inducing counterfeit passion.

But the most ingenious was 'The Bed of Unrelinquishable Torment'.

The bishop had been most impressed by the pose in which we had to take our corrective exercises, kneeling with widespread legs on the arms of the sturdy armchair that had once adorned papa's study, and now did the same for that of the judge. He had commented that an awkward pose contributed to the effort a girl had to make to maintain her position, much to the good of her soul, but that occasionally, it could be beneficial if she were made helpless before the flagellation proceeded.

'Strap them down, d'ye mean?' the judge asked. 'Could be a useful variant, I suppose.'

'Indeed,' the right reverend gentleman agreed. 'And there are more subtle methods, too. A young woman may be most elegantly placed, and endure the most stringent punishment, and yet not seem anxious to escape or shield her person. If you like I can demonstrate the effect on my next visit.'

As has already been recorded, the bishop was now a regular diner and there was but little time passed before we were welcoming him again. When we women had cleared the table, and reported to the study in our usual state of undress, we found a new piece of furniture had been added.

It was a bench, long and low, beautifully constructed and decorated, with mother of pearl inlays, a lacquered finish, and various elegant and interesting cut-outs and curlicues to break up the stark outlines of a simple bench. But, under it all, the careful eye could still see it was a sturdy construction.

'Though I know it has been the custom of the house that the eldest sister should demonstrate each new piece of apparatus first, I have a fancy for my own special charge, Annabelle, to make first assay of the device,' the bishop observed.

'I see no objection,' the judge ruled. 'Indeed, there is at least one precedent, I recall. When the branks was first introduced by our good friend the doctor, it was the clack-tongued Charlotte that tasted it first.'

Charlotte hung her head in shame at the recollection. It was noticeable how much less forward in her speech she had become since the doctor paid his visit to Scotland, and returned bearing the hideous contraption of steel and iron known as the scold's bridle, or branks.

Thus it was that I was first summoned to mount the bench. I was made to lie, face down, along its length and to pull myself along until my breasts, half hanging out of my stays in this posture, fell into two of the curious cut-outs, painted and inlaid to represent the mouths of fat exotic fishes. Then I must part my legs to let them lie along the sides of the bench, my sex directly over another of the openings, this time fashioned as the long gaping mouth of a great dragon coiled along the bench between my knees.

I lay still, as ordered, my arms stretched in front of me along the lacquered surface. Suddenly I started, and was immediately told to stay still. Something had moved in the space beneath my left breast and touched the nipple which, to my shame, stiffened at the contact. It was for all the world as if the fish had begun to suckle on the teat, though I subsequently learnt it was but a tube, on the other end of which a bellows pulled, drawing in the fleshy stub. With my breast now drawn fully out of my stays and into the recess, I gasped again, for tiny teeth, the serrated jaws of a metal clamp, had seized the nipple at its base, and held it tight. Now the mechanism drew on my right teat until it too had been secured by the teeth below the bench.

I cannot describe the strange feelings of terror and excitement mixed that this outlandish restraint induced in me, but I had more to come.

Something rose from the dragon's mouth, forcing itself into the tight slit between my pouting sex lips, as if the dragon was using its tongue to salute me there. Then its jaws closed on either side, trapping the lips against the tongue. Those jaws were equipped with short, needle-sharp teeth, which gripped my tender flesh, piercing the skin to the depth of a fingernail's thickness only, but set to drag themselves ever deeper the more I resisted their pull.

Clenched together around my captive vulva, the dragon's jaws withdrew, and my sex with it, pinning me to the bench.

Picture me then, my breasts gripped in the mouths of

Pisces, my sex in the locked dragon-jaws. I lay on the bench, my arms free, my legs free, but totally captive, unless, that is, I cared to drag my most intimate parts from their traps, scouring the skin from them in the process, and much of the tissue besides. No wonder it was described as unrelinquishable!

In this position I received twenty cuts from the judge's most potent rod, cuts that had me writhing and whining on the bench, trying to endure as best I could. I clasped the bench under me with my arms, holding my breasts tightly into the ravenous mouths of the fishes, lest I inadvertently pull on them in my agony and tear the tender dugs. I would have liked to have dropped my knees either side of the bench and gripped tight there also, but to do so would have canted up my pelvis, and the dragon would not permit it, sinking his vicious teeth deeper into those fleshy lips at even a thought of withdrawal. And I must lie with my legs along the bench, straight out behind me, bunching up my nether cheeks so that the cane might penetrate into their base with ease.

It was a masterpiece of ingenuity, appreciating a woman's response exactly, leaving her bound, yet free of the comforting security of bondage, which females will use to reduce the exercise of fortitude that is such an essential part of the rehabilitative process inherent in their correction.

Navigation

The summer that year proved to be both long and hot. Though in some degree welcome, my sisters and I did find it troublesome in many ways. Our tight corseting and the many fetters and other restraints we wore from time to time to curb our youthful exuberance, and the discomfort that caused our male guardians.

Indeed, the effects were amplified by the influence of the heat, and our female effusions so much exaggerated by the warmth of the season, which resulted in their having to call upon our services more and more frequently. Our poor fundaments became quite sore from the so frequent reaming they suffered, day and night, the soreness bought to our consciousness even when most diverted by cleansing labour as our perspiration trickled down our backs and sought out the deep creases of our buttocks and the tender anuses that lay within.

It was with some pleasure therefore, that we learnt from the gentlemen that they planned to make an excursion across country, possibly to the metropolis itself, if time permitted, enjoying the benefits of the passenger carrying barges that had recently come into use and that, moreover, we would have the privilege of accompanying them. We busied ourselves with packing and preparation in a mood of some excitement. Our own preparations, naturally, did not occupy us long, having only the barest of possessions and, thankfully, spared those anxieties and decisions that so beset females burdened with extensive wardrobes and multiple choices of outfits from which to select what they might pack for the voyage. But we were occupied for some time in ironing, starching folding polishing sewing and darning, to ensure that each gentleman was equipped as suited his station, and would not go without those necessary changes of garment and daily fresh linen that their rank called for.

Eventually all was ready, and we were all conveyed by carriage to the basin on the canal where our vessel lay, and our voyage would commence.

We were delighted with the craft, so carefully designed, so well constructed, with fittings of teak and copper, ingenious closets for clothing and for hygiene. Even a kitchen, or galley as we learnt to call it, with a very convenient iron stove in which to prepare the gentlemen's meals, when they did not repair to some waterside hostelry, with which the waterways were, we discovered, liberally provided.

We carried the gentlemen's portmanteaus on board and hung up their clothes, set out their toilet articles and generally made things as comfortable for them as the restricted, but luxurious accommodation permitted. The one thing that seemed to be lacking was a horse to propel the barge, and barge-man to supervise its labours.

The latter omission was rectified when a stocky red-faced brute of a man appeared and asked our guardians if they were ready to depart. They agreed that they were set, but still there was no sign of a horse. It was at this point that our true function, apart from our normal duties from seeing to the gentlemen's wants of all kinds, was explained to us. It appeared that the doctor had suggested that it would be excellent for our health if we were to act as draught animals on the trip, the exercise being beneficial to our bodies and souls, a sentiment that we could not in reason object to. We were, however, a little dismayed at the manner in which we were to be employed. Since our efforts would inevitably result in our perspiring, not to say sweat profusely, and the towropes would tend to abrade our shoulders, we would undertake the task without our gowns, clad only in our stays and petticoats. We understood the reasoning well enough, but were somewhat embarrassed by the thought of appearing bare-breasted in a public place, for the design of our stays was such that they did nothing to cover out bosoms which would be totally exposed, even calling attention to themselves by the flashing of the large gold rings we wore in our teats.

When we respectfully drew attention to this fact we were admonished for lack of obedience, and promised some extra discipline at the appropriate time for questioning their decision. We should not think of ourselves, we were told, as women, while carrying out this duty, but as draught animals. Indeed, we would be expected to refrain from speech while engaged on towing duty. Moreover, in keeping with our role of substitute horses, we would find our forms decorated in much the same way as the animals we replaced. And in particular, would be given small bells to attach to our nipple rings, which would give out a merry jingle as we progressed through the countryside. With this information and admonishment we were sent to strip and prepare for duty.

We duly appeared on the quayside, clad in petticoats and stays. Our barge-master looked us over and drew attention to our boots and stocking.

'There's always clartey patches along the towpath,' he remarked. 'And the mud will spoil those fine boots. Moreover there's places, this dry weather, where it's a mite dusty, too. Best go barefoot, I'm thinking. Leave them on the gunnel. One of you can attend to them later.'

The gunwale, we understood, was the rim of the boat and, since it had been made plain that this uncompromising creature was to be in complete charge of us and, moreover, carried a most unpleasant-looking whip coiled under his arm, we made haste to obey lest we feel its bite on our bare shoulders or, worse, our shamefully exposed breasts.

We were to pull the boat by means of a substantial towrope attached to a post in the front of the barge and extending to the shore, where it terminated in the centre of a triangular iron-plate wooden bar from whose corners three shorter ropes hung. We were each to pull on a rope, passed over one shoulder and fastened around our waists.

There was, however, a hidden refinement to this form of harness.

While the rope gave the appearance of merely circling our waists it did, in fact, pass under the waistband in front and pass between our legs before traversing the divide of our buttocks to actually circle our middles from behind. This was no great matter so long as we were fresh enough, and our arms retained enough strength to pull on the rope directly. But any slipping in that endeavour and the pull was transferred to our tender cunnies and fundaments, with salutary results in terms of incentive to try harder.

The three of us were harnessed in a troika of femininity; Marion at the 'point', Charlotte and I to either side. Our rubicund taskmaster cracked his whip menacingly above our heads and growled, 'Giddup,' and we leant against the ropes and strove to set the heavy barge in motion.

Little by little it began to move as we strained at our ropes. It will readily be seen that, if all three were to make equal effort the pull on the three corners of the iron-plate would be in balance, and the plate stay square to the towrope. But if one of us were to do less than her share, the plate would tilt in one direction or another and the culprit be revealed. Our driver, for what else might one call him, utilised this simple device to accord us cuts of his whip in accordance with our effort. The lash was not heavy, but stung exceedingly, cutting the flesh if he became urgent in his message, or angry with our failings, and we soon learned to dread its bite.

We flung ourselves into the task and were soon rewarded by the slow acceleration of the craft from where it had been moored, out into the channel. We were off, but still we were urged on by bite of tongue and lash. We reached a walking pace, then a marching gait. The day was already hot and perspiration had started almost with our first efforts, and now we streamed.

Still our driver would not let us relax, and drove us on until we were stepping out in a smart jog. Only then did he cease to pressure us with growls and the crack of his cutting lash on our tender bare shoulders and breasts. We hurt so much already, and had gained such an instant dislike of that biting lash, that we did not for an instant let our pace drop but, once the barge had reached a sought for speed it was surprisingly easy to maintain it.

We jogged along much more easily now, our motion making the bells in our teats ring out merrily, warning any around of our coming, and drawing their attention to our shameful nudity and demeaning employment.

Our pace established, our driver moved to where the three ropes came together at the triangle and called on Marion to easy, while warning Charlotte and I not to let the pace drop. He then unhooked her rope from the plate, which had turned on its side, with only two of us attached and pulling and sent her to board the boat.

The bishop who, it turned out, was a man of more practicality than the spiritual nature of his calling might suggest, was at the tiller, and brought the sleek craft close enough to the bank that she could jump aboard. With only two of us now to share the work, Charlotte and I found ourselves sweating freely once more as we took up the load. It was not long before our backs were aching with the strain, and our tender bare feet cut and sore from the dustier and gravel-strewn parts of the path, muddied and fouled from the wetter patches and the dung dropped by those four-legged draught animals that had preceded us. We did not dare slacken, however, for even the slightest diminution of our pace and our driver sought out our most tender parts for the attention of that whipcord lash that so tormented our soft flesh. An easement of my effort to favour my sore shoulder, and it cut into my back like a knife, a hesitation or stumble, and the thong wrapped itself around my chest and bit up into the tenderness of my teats, wrenching an involuntary squeal from my panting lungs.

For over half an hour we proceeded in this manner until, truly distressed, we were called on to walk then halt as the boat slowly lost way and slid into the bank. We dropped to our knees and rested in the mud, regardless of our skirts, only thankful to be spared the labour and the lash, if only temporarily, for we were under no illusions that this was just a short halt.

In our distress we had forgotten Marion, but now she reappeared to aid us in getting the heavy craft in motion again. With a little experience now, the three of us soon had it moving and worked it up to the jog trot that had been set as our cruising speed. We dare not think of what would be implied by the need for more swift progress, then Marion left us again to return to her duties aboard the floating home.

As time passed we found that the pattern of our lives of this outing involved the harnessing of all three to get the boat underway, then the release of she who had the 'point' at departure, to serve the gentlemen's needs aboard. When my turn came I was made to put my attire and my person into what order I could, then provide the gentlemen with drinks against the heat – we trailed both wine and beer in bottles over the stern where the water kept them cool – and to prepare sufficient meals to keep their pangs of hunger at bay, besides putting up bread and water for the 'dray horses' for their midday break.

Such culinary duty in the galley was interrupted from time to time when I had to strip again and take my turn on the rope, when it became time to restart the journey. Besides all this, there were calls throughout the day from one or other of our guardians who felt the influence of such strong female exertions, and their resultant secretions, so unsettling that nothing would serve but to have his bodily fluids drained. Several times that day I was made to fall to my knees and take a turgid member into my mouth, using those skills we had all three acquired by now to coax from the rigid shafts the pernicious effusions occasioned by our sinful presence. With tutored feathering by tongue and teeth, and graduated suckling of the purple glans, we were now able to guarantee to bring even the most reluctant and spent organ to ejaculate its evil load into our mouths, where we would swallow it wholly and immediately to ensure it could do no further harm.

Sometimes one of the guardians would feel he would need to participate more actively in this drainage of his system and call upon us to expose our buttocks and part the cheeks to present access to our anal buds. With the limited size and layout of our floating home, this was usually most convenient to him if we knelt on the steps, or companionway as we later learnt was the correct term, that led down into the saloon, bring our rear passage to optimum height for our guardian's comfort, and leaving him in the privacy of the cabin. Of course, this meant that I was quite exposed to public gaze during the procedure and it added to my embarrassment more than somewhat that, during those moments when, perforce, a girl must pant and howl as the spasm mounts within her, I was subject to the gaze of those on passing boats, girls taking the air along the towpath with their swains, or rude and licentious bragees. It was the females of the latter class that brought the hottest blushes to my cheek. It is certain they had no doubts whatever as to what was passing and would call out loudly, encouraging me to, 'Go to it, girl. Milk that pole. Grip it with your guts, Missy. Suck him dry and try another.' Such coarse behaviour, so inappropriate to the nobility of the service we were rendering, was especially galling.

It may be remarked however that we were not the only females to be used in this manner while kneeling on the companionway. We observed in our travels that many a man might use his woman so when the need came upon him, the female continuing the pilotage of the boat, which glided forward under the patient pull of the horse on the bank, the woman steering by reaching out for the tiller from her bent position, and guiding the craft by watching its wake behind. Another example of the triumph of the human will over the demands of our animal nature.

Nor was our service to our guardians the only kind we were called upon to make. At each lock, and they were many after the first stretch of waterway, for they did at least allow for a break in the intolerable towing, we were set to put our sore backs against the great timber beams to close and open the gates, and to bend and crank to raise and lower the paddles that controlled the flow of water into the basin, to raise the boat to a new level. In doing so we relieved the lock keeper of much of his duty, but he still seemed to expect a tip or *pour boire*.

On the first occasion the judge called out, 'I've no small change, my man, but you may take your dues from one of those pretty arses if you will. Bum only, mind. Touch their cunts and I'll see you hanged.'

We were most touched that he should take such trouble to preserve our virginities, but it was still somewhat of a trial to have to submit our fundaments to strangers. With our own guardians we were used to the practice, understood the need for it and, moreover, while in no way guilty of undue indulgence of us, their familiarity with our bodies, and we with theirs, led to a certain easiness in the congress, which was totally lacking in the rude and brutal way in which we were taken on these casual conjoinings.

The first time I was selected for this service, the lock keeper, a huge and brutal fellow in a sweat-stained shirt and rough woollen trousers, hauled me unceremoniously into the tiny hut that served him on the lock-side, only a flimsy plank door separating us from the curious onlookers outside. There he forced me over until I was bent almost touching my toes, and flipped my petticoats over my head, exposing my pale round buttocks. He slapped them familiarly with a broad coarse palm, callused by his trade, and grunted that it was nice meat and worth a poke. His great thumbs plunged into the gully between my nether cheeks and brutally tore them asunder, so roughly that I grunted loud enough to be heard outside, and I heard answering jeers and calls from those who waited without. Then I screamed in earnest for, without the slightest preparation, not even an application of his foul saliva, distasteful as that might have been, he thrust himself deep into me in one furious heave. The man was immense. Our guardians, though a trifle too well-endowed about the belly and thighs perhaps, were well-set-up men with considerable members, of which they might not be ashamed in any company, but this brute put them all to shade.

He was ramming me in furious assault, my howls echoed by the ribald mirth of the crowd outside. It was as well perhaps that my nether orifice was regularly put to the prick, for I am sure matters would have gone very badly for me else. Even so, sick and nauseous as I was, I could still feel that rising tide of sensation that seemed to accompany the approach of the male discharge. The only saving grace I could find in the monster was that he was quick. As suddenly as he had started, he erupted in great gouts of fluid which I could distinctly feel as they impinged on my intestinal walls. And then he was gone, wiping his dripping member on my petticoat and unceremoniously throwing open the door of the hut, leaving me bent bare-buttocked, the spent juices dribbling from my anus.

I hastily gathered myself together and sought to flee the public gaze, but it was not to be. Our driver called out that it was time to move and to take up our places for the tow, and for the next ten minutes or so, until we had moved away from the lock area, I had to endure the derision and coarse advice of the crowd.

As we became used to the hard work, and the shameful indignity of our near nudity, we began to observe that we were not the only human draught animals on the 'cut', as the canal was universally known. It would appear that quite a number of bargees were either so poor, or so mean, that they had no horse and employed their spouses for the task. We came across many such, often aided by their daughters when of age enough, and often but little better covered than ourselves, though it would appear by reason of want rather than a conscious act, although it may be that they preferred to keep their only gown in good repair and suffer exposure to lewd gazes and inclement weather as we did.

Nor was maternity any bar to such employment, and there were several swollen bellies amongst those set to tow the barges.

As I have remarked, we became accustomed to the work, though it never became easy, and our high stepping trot was much faster than the steady trudge expected from the women working on their own. Nor did the humiliation of our jingling bells soften with time, and a day came which brought a further trial.

We had reached the mouth of the notorious Sitrim tunnel; three miles of dark, dank oppressive rock hewn passage, where no path was provided for towers, whether of the four or two-legged variety. The boats were propelled through by 'legging', that is by lying on our backs on planks set either side of the bow, and pressing our feet against the tunnel lining. By walking in mid-air, so to speak, the boat was made to move. Once the planks were in place we were ordered to remove our remaining clothing, and to undertake the duty stark naked, it being pointed out that the drips from the slimy roof would ruin our garb and that, in any case, in the confines of the tunnel there would be none to see us.

Accordingly, we found ourselves lying on our backs on hard planking, walking on a rock face in our bare feet, the surface carrying numerous sharp projections left over from its cutting, which plagued our tender soles, partly covered with a loathsome layer of stinking slime. This slime extended over the entire roof and, loosened by the water that seeped through the canopy, fell in large and frequent gobs onto the boat and we who lay on it, the gentlemen very properly not exposing their valuable selves and raiment, and sheltering in the saloon. Since we were quite naked and lying on our backs, many of these unpleasant droppings fell directly on us and even found the aperture of our opening thighs and assaulted our most intimate parts.

The tunnel was over three miles in length and we were nearly two hours traversing it, and arrived at the far end most uncomfortably bespattered, for which we were roundly reprimanded by our guardians and unceremoniously dunked in the water of the cut to cleanse us. We were judged to be too wet to resume even that little clothing we were normally allowed, and completed the next hour's tow quite naked still. Luckily there were few to see us on that isolated stretch, other than the ubiquitous bargees who made clear in what direction their lecherous thoughts were moved by our nudity.

Charlotte was so ill advised as to protest at this affront to our modesty, being made to run naked like an animal. It proved a costly indiscretion for the gentlemen at once judged her guilty of mutiny, and the judge sentenced her on the spot to be flogged at the mast, by which he meant the stout post that served as an anchorage for the tow. Being naked already there was little delay, and she was triced up by her wrists, only her toes touching the deck. There was, however, sufficient time for the word to be shouted all along the towpath in both directions.

'A flogging, a flogging. There's a young bitch about to get her back warmed,' and a considerable crowd had assembled by the time she was taut in place, and the driver, to whom the duty had been delegated, positioned behind her.

He had secured from somewhere – I learnt later he had borrowed from one of the other boats where equine propulsion was employed – a long narrow leather trace that served as an excellent whip, the thin lash he employed to drive us being too long and unwieldy for the close confines of the boat's deck. With this he proceeded to lay on the fifty lashes to which poor Charlotte had been condemned.

She made a picture of beauty as she hung from her hands at the post, her long white back but faintly marked from the urgings of the thin lash previously, her delicate waist flaring out to sleek but womanly hips, the rounded buttocks tight and firm from their being so well-exercised in towage. The post guarded her mossy grove in front, but her firm pert breasts pressed proudly out either side of the rough timber pole, which rubbed the tender valley between quite sorely.

All thoughts of such discomfort, and the stress on her

wrists and toes as she hung in place, vanished with the first crack of the lash on her pale shoulders. She gasped and tensed as if taken aback by the force of the blow and the sting of its attack, then grunted again as the second fell a little lower. With remorseless precision the blows progressed down her back to the jut of her buttocks, laid on with sufficient pause for her to benefit entirely from each, but fast enough to keep her constantly fighting to maintain some control. Women will always fight these battles, and as frequently lose them. By the time the lash had completed the first ladder of stripes and started down again from the top, she was screaming freely, her shrieks echoed by the laughter of the barge folk who had gathered to watch.

The women were even worse in their behaviour than the men. It might be thought that they would display some sympathy for one of their own sex subjected to such a whipping. Such scenes were not uncommon of the cut as we had already observed on several occasions, but their own experiences and fears, far from calling forth their kinder natures, seemed only to bring out the harshest and most cruel reactions.

The women danced and howled on the bank, calling for poor Charlotte to be whipped more, mocking the driver that he was no man if he did not make her howl, promising him, in the coarsest terms, the delights of their own bodies if he should achieve what they so evidently desired. By the end of her fifty strokes poor Charlotte did indeed hang sobbing in her bonds, but whether the driver collected on the offers made I cannot tell.

It would seem, however, that the correction was successful in its purpose as Charlotte did not raise her eyes from the ground for days afterwards, even when on the tow, for she was not excused above a day from that duty, and had to haul the cruel rope over shoulders but newly wealed and sore.

We women are nothing if not resilient though, and within days were all back in our usual spirits and beginning to enjoy the life, whose hardships were little more than our daily domestic duties at home and which enabled us to breathe the fresh air and take in the warmth of the sun in the delightful countryside through which we passed.

And we were not alone in that environment. A constant stream of traffic on the water demonstrated the prosperity that the land was enjoying. This traffic to some extent accompanied us, for although we made better progress while on the move, the efforts of two trotting girls being enough to move our lightly laden craft faster than the deeply loaded barges, the latter did not take those long breaks for refreshment at the hostelries along the way that our guardians found so essential to the roving life. Thus we kept re-encountering many of the barge people. Though some were friendly, many of the women, particularly the older ones, seemed jealous of our youthful health and privileged station in life, and manifested this envy by denouncing the nudity we wore when towing as shameful and an offence to other females.

As time went by they formed a coherent band of furies that screamed abuse at us whenever we appeared at locks or passing places, until one evening matters came to a head at an inn, where we had stopped and where we had been put outside while the gentlemen enjoyed the last of their meal inside.

Thus unprotected we were easy prey to the parcel of drunken barge women that suddenly erupted from the taproom and surrounded us.

'Sluts, whores, jezebels!' they screamed in their drunken fury. 'String 'em up, rip their cunts, stuff their arses!' they shrieked, and we cringed before them. Never have I seen such rampant evil as those who still called themselves women but were unworthy to be named members of that sex.

Then, 'Caulk their cunts,' one suggested. 'That'll keep our men out of their sin pits,' and someone called for tar, and others rushed to the boatyard nearby and came back with a great smoking pot of hot black semi-fluid that was used to stop the cracks between the planking of the boats.

Now it was our cracks it would seal!

We were no match for these hardened harridans of the cut, and in moments were bent backwards over the bench on which we sat. Rough hands grasped our legs and raised and parted them, letting our petticoats fall about our hips and exposing us shamefully to the public gaze. It is a curious thing that I never felt so humiliated or shamed before men, no matter how gross the circumstances of my exposure, as I did before these women. Somehow there was a naturalness in one's person being bare before men, part of the natural order of things, while exposure to females seemed a perversion of that healthy norm. Of course, I was used to being open with my sisters, but that

189

was a different matter altogether, done in circumstances of love and sisterly feeling.

I had little time enough for these speculations as the howling harpies tore my legs apart and the searing heat of the tar brush found the quivering cunny between. I shrieked in pain and despair as the hot tar penetrated my crack, seeming to fill my belly, though I later discovered it barely passed the outer lips. My thick bush of dark hair that covered my woman's parts fared less well. The viscose matter froze onto the curled tendrils and converted all to a tough black mat, immovable by any normal means and impenetrable to testing tongue or finger.

Apart from the hurt of the hot tar, something a woman may endure and dismiss soon enough, we were plagued by being denied entirely that solace to which we resorted to alleviate the troubles of the day and the smart of our stripes. The material, when it set, became such a tough carapace, reinforced as it was by our nether hair, that all access to our sensitive buds was impossible and we must lie in frustration until it could be removed. We had no facilities for this on our tour and it was not until we returned home that we could relieve ourselves of the unwelcome addition to our anatomies, and then only at the expense of the sacrifice of our lower hair, which must be pulled out at the roots.

For Charlotte, whose pubic decoration was more fuzz than fur, this was no great torment. But both Marion and myself were endowed with luxuriant thickets of tight glossy curls that adhered the tar without hope of separation, and whose extraction was torture of a particularly unbearable and long-lasting kind. We were both in tears before we had managed to remove the bulk of our contamination, and were not truly clean for months.

It was fortunate perhaps that this unhappy incident took place towards the end of our cruise. Naturally enough, seeing what orifice the gentlemen made use of in draining their humours, we were able to be of our usual service to them, but became increasingly morose and unhappy from being denied our own relief, and were much improved once we had returned home and torn the offending tar from our bodies.

It should not be thought that we had not enjoyed our time on the cut, despite the hardships endured, for novelty is always welcome. If anyone came home in lower spirits than she had left it was Charlotte, who took her flogging very heavily, being much removed for a time from her usual buoyant self, not looking the gentlemen in the eye and only speaking when spoken to. It is a well-known fact that, for women, a flogging on the back is a much harder affair to bear than a whipping on any other part. A woman's buttocks are so intimately connected to her belly that it is almost inevitable that sensations created in the one, however painful, will be transmitted to the other, and as inevitable that the womb will convert them to the only sense it is created for; pleasure of the most carnal sort. Even the breasts or the cunny, though so much more sensitive, will to a degree effect this mutation of pain into pleasure when transmitting it to the seat of womanhood. As the doctor was fond of remarking when discoursing on the subject, 'In a woman, all roads lead to womb.'

The Dignity of Labour

It was about this time that we received another visitor. At dinner one night we were surprised to find not three gentlemen, but four, our guardians having been joined by a large gentleman of florid appearance. His manner was abrupt, as if brooking of no opposition, and he radiated an aura of power and ruthlessness that caused us females to quiver internally, and treat him with even greater respect than due in any case to a member of his sex.

'This is Mr Brangwyn,' the judge informed us, by way of introduction. 'He will be staying a day or two. Kindly lay an extra place and see that there is a room made up for him.'

Naturally we hastened to comply, then served the meal, each kneeling, as usual, beside her particular guardian to receive from their plates and glasses such sustenance and refreshment as they chose to allow us.

Mr Brangwyn seemed much impressed by the procedure, though in truth, we found it now the most natural thing in the world, and commented freely on how well we had been trained, and the high degree of submission that our guardians had induced in us.

'I only wish,' he said, 'that the idle bitches who work for me were half as docile.'

His speech, it must be admitted, was rather on the coarse side, compared with the educated and enlightened conversation of the others. But we put that down to too long exposure to the uneducated and brutal labourers he employed, for Mr Brangwyn was the proprietor of several collieries in the Forest of Dean, on the English-Welsh border.

After dinner it was time for the regular disciplinary exercises. It would have normally been Charlotte's turn to account for her sins, and service the gentlemen's needs but, in honour of our guest, we were each required to strip to the usual degree, and mount the chair for our buttocks to be scourged and our souls purged, before easing the executioner of our penance, by the actions of our nether orifices clenching around their inflamed members.

We were a little taken aback, at fist, to find Mr Brangwyn accompanying us to the study, where the process was to be carried out. But it was made clear to us that industry was to join religion, medicine and the law in our governance, in accordance with the most modern thinking, and we forbore to argue with our betters on the matter.

Thus it was that, after I had received a particularly severe whipping from the bishop, who seemed to have abrogated the usual formula for their calculation, and thrashed me so sorely that I could not hold back my tears, not only he but our new guardian entered me from behind, squeezing my sore nether cheeks with hard male hands, while their iron-hard rods reamed my tender back passage.

I was more than ready for my bed that night, and some tears stained my pillow.

The coal magnate stayed with us three days, with three nights of exceptional soreness as we demonstrated how far the limits of our endurance stretched. He seemed to rejoice in our restraints, as being so beneficial to womankind, and would often come at first light to see us cavort naked under the icy pump, apparently greatly approving of this means to hygiene of body and soul.

Thereafter he became a regular visitor, and we were always in a state of particular apprehension when one of these visits was announced, for we knew that our discipline would acquire an extra dimension of strictness and depth, while he was with us.

On one such occasion we were warned in advance that he was coming to take us back with him to Monmouthshire. Since we might be away for some weeks, we thought the gentlemen might have refused his request, for we had, in our arrogant female pride, come to feel we were essential to their health and comfort. But they assured us they would make shift without our services, and had already made suitable arrangements to cover our absence.

It was for our own good we were being sent, they assured us, to learn the dignity of labour and the benefits of toil, and they would make the best of things while we were absent, so that we might not miss the opportunity offered.

We travelled in the gentleman's own carriage, staying the first night in Salisbury, where I was deputed to visit his room to remove the harmful accretions occasioned by his close proximity to us in the coach, then arrived very late in Bath the following evening, where we stopped the night, Charlotte being his choice of remedy for the excessive pressure visible in his britches from long confinement within an arm's length of three fertile females.

We saw nothing of the city that might once have been our home, to the great danger of our moral health, no doubt, a fate from which we had saved ourselves by persuading the judge to take us under his hand.

The next day we crossed to Chepstow on the ferry and proceeded to the hall, set in parkland, where Mr Brangwyn resided. It came as somewhat of a surprise that, during those last few miles, when we were in country where he was the local squire, and well known, the folk along the way greeted the carriage with sullen looks and muttered curses. We were moved to comment on this to our host, but he dismissed it, saying the local people were a surly breed, and to ignore them.

Marion extracted his malign juices that night, and in the morning we were to have our first experience of industrial labour. We speculated among ourselves what form it might take, for Mr Brangwyn had given us no inkling of what he intended for us, and we had been specifically enjoined by our guardians to ask no questions of him, but to display that total obedience to all commands, to which we had been trained.

We left the house before dawn, for we understood work started early. As the carriage passed along the street of mean houses where the workers lived, there were many of them along the way. They shouted and shook their fists at us, the women worst of all, screaming insults, calling us whores and scabs, though we had little understanding of what they were about. Again our host advised us to take no notice.

'These are idle folk, who will not work,' he said. 'Nor

195

listen to the wisdom of their betters, both by rank and gender.'

We felt sorrow that women could so demean our sex, and determined that we, at least, would do nothing to disgrace womankind, resolving to obey implicitly, and to work as hard as our female frames permitted.

We were taken to the mine adit, a shed with a windlass worked by patient horses, that lowered wheeled tubs down into the pit, to fetch the coal, and hoisted them out after, when filled.

It appeared the workers, as well as the coals, travelled this route, and there was just room in the cage for the three of us to stand together. Mr Brangwyn addressed us before the windlass was released.

'There is no room for me to accompany you further,' he said, 'but the overseer will be waiting at the pit bottom. You are to obey him, as myself, and not to question anything he orders, however surprising. Everything that is done is for the safety of the mine, and the health of the workers. It is a pity that the idle women whose place you are taking, do not understand this. I look to you to show a better sense of a woman's duty and place.'

With that he signalled to the man at the windlass, who let the brake loosen, and the swaying platform on which we stood fell below our feet, dropping us into the shaft.

The motion was so sudden, unexpected and swift, we screamed as one woman. In pitch darkness we plunged into the depths, shrieking like lost souls. Indeed, at the time we thought ourselves just that, doomed and on our way to hell. Nor were we altogether wrong in our assessment, though it was a hell quite beyond any of our imaginings.

After what seemed an age the cage began to slow, as the winch-man applied the brake, and our feet pressed as strongly against the floor as they had lightened as we fell. The motion almost ceased, and we became aware of a faint light as we dangled on the thread of rope that was all that held us from being dashed to the ground below.

As the cage steadied and came to a halt, we found ourselves at an opening in the side of the rock-lined shaft, lit by flickering lamps on either side, whose light seemed only to make more black the cavern, grimed as it was with coal dust, which lay everywhere and entered everything. Standing in the entrance to this fearful tunnel was a man, the overseer we had been promised, we assumed.

He was short but broad, very powerful, his coarse features ingrained with coal, dressed in thick woollen trousers, heavy boots, and a dirty collar-less shirt. His head was wound about with a cloth, over which he wore a flat cap, presumably as some protection for impact with the roof of the workings, for the tunnel, after the relatively wide space at the pit bottom for handling of tubs and workers, shrank to no more than a yard high by two wide, just enough for the tubs to pass on their way to and from the coal face.

He peered at us in the dim light of the lamps, and an evil grin came onto his face.

'So you're the scabs he promised,' he said. 'Well, what's keeping you? Off with them.'

We must have looked totally bemused by this, for he went on.

'Women don't work clothed down here,' he told us. 'Too hot, and their skirts get in the way. Besides, you'd never get all clean again, with so much petticoats and such. Come now, quick. Get all that gear off and hurry up about it.'

We looked at each other in shock. It was Marion, the eldest and clearest headed as usual who recovered first.

'We must do as he asks,' she said. 'I can see some sense in what he says and, more importantly, we have our orders. We are to obey him without question, so we must strip and get ourselves ready for the work.'

We each removed our outer clothing, our dresses, our underslips, our petticoats. When we stood in a state of almost total undress, merely stays, stockings and shoes, in accordance with our long-standing custom we wore no drawers of any kind, we instinctively paused, feeling that this must be enough. The overseer, seeing us stopped, said nothing but unbuckled the heavy leather strap from around his waist. Still without a word, he lashed it across Marion's thighs, then Charlottes, finally my own.

'Are you deaf or daft?' he exclaimed. 'When I say stripped, I mean as nature made you. Every last thing off, and as bare as a slug in the rain. That's how the women work here. Let's have no more delay, or you'll get more than just a touch of my belt.'

In no doubts now of what he required, and the desirability of meeting his requirements, we tore off the last of our clothing and stood before him in the state he demanded.

198

'That's better,' he conceded, and proceeded to buckle a wide strap about each of our waists, for all the world like the girths used on dray horses, pulling up tight on the twin buckles until they were tight about our hips.

He led us over to where some empty tubs waited at the bottom of the shaft.

'Kneel,' he said, and we dropped to our knees before him. From the front of each belt a length of heavy chain fell, with a hook at its end. He thrust Marion's head down until she went on all fours, and reached between her legs from behind to grasp the hook, pulling the chain through her parted thighs and dropping the hook into a ring on the front of one of the wheeled tubs.

He treated Charlotte and I in the same way. I could not help cringing from the feel of his coal-grimed hairy wrist brushing against my vulva, as he reached between my thighs, and he laughed evilly.

'Touched your private purse, did I, my little darling? I'll do more than touch one of these days.'

I shuddered, but made no reply.

When we were all hooked up to tubs, he ordered Marion to crawl on her hands and knees into the entrance of the narrow tunnel, then Charlotte and I were formed into line behind her.

'Crawl down the passage, and keep right on going until you reach lights,' he ordered. 'Keep to the left-hand side, in case there are men or tubs coming the other way. You'll find men working and loaded tubs where the lights are. The men will unhook your chains from the empty tubs and fasten them to full ones, which you will pull back here. You go on doing that until someone tells you to stop.

'Off you go,' he cried, and brought the strap down heavily across Marion's rump.

She started forward, came up short as the chain tensioned, then threw herself against the weight to get the clumsy vehicle moving on its crude wheels. As she entered the narrow darkness of the tunnel, the overseer brought the strap down on Charlotte's bottom in silent command and she gasped and threw her weight against her own tub. No sooner had she started to move after Marion's disappearing form, than the cruel strap lashed into my own bent buttocks, and I suppressed a cry to hurl myself against the belt and get my tub moving before he thought I might need more encouragement.

Though the tub was crude and clumsy, it was empty and the tunnel ran downhill, so at the beginning at least the task was not overwhelming and, in fact, there were times when the tub would overrun one, catching one's ankles painfully. The floor of the tunnel was relatively smooth, from the continuous polishing by countless female knees and palms, but hard, with the occasional fragment of coal to torment one's kneecaps or soft hands.

We ploughed on in pitch darkness, once we had left the pit bottom a few yards behind, kept in touch by the rumbling of the trucks in front or behind.

It was hot and airless in the tunnel and we were soon sweating like the draught animals we were. We crawled painfully on for what seemed hours before we caught the first loom of light beyond where the tunnel curved a little in front, then came to another slightly wider portion, with two lamps burning, and a number of near-naked men working the coal with picks, by the dim light they provided. At first they seemed oblivious to our presence, merely cursing us for not getting there earlier, saying the tubs were full long ago and they were losing time. Then they looked closer and began to exchange remarks.

'Not the usual lasses then,' one commented.

'Nay,' his companion agreed. 'These look as if they've been washed not long ago,' though how they could tell, since the coal dust had clung to every part of our sweat-soaked bodies, I could not imagine at the time. The women they usually saw down there must have been blackened indeed.

But it was not long before I found out in my own person, just how much blacker one could get.

The men dropped their picks and hurried over to unhitch the empty trucks and fasten us to new, taking advantage of their tasks to pass callused coal-blackened hands over our pubes and our dangling breasts, making no pretence of anything but lust as an excuse for their actions. One of them evidently admired large breasts on a woman, for he fondled Marion's generous endowment at length.

'Dugs on this one like a milker,' he told his mates. 'Make a nice place for a man to rest his head, eh Dai?'

'These are the pillows for me,' Dai answered, slapping me none too gently on the buttocks. 'There's a tight little seam I wouldn't mind working.'

'Mind what you're about,' another warned him. 'Get them too swollen to work, and you'll find Evan Overseer after you.'

'Oh, there's more ways of skinning a cat than filling its belly with kittens,' Dai laughed. 'There's a little pit here just waiting to be mined, and no babies squawling at the bottom, either,' and I squealed and jerked forward as a rough finger invaded my tender anus.

'No time for that sort of play,' their leader said. 'We've got a stint to complete. And you bitches, get that coal to the shaft and be quick about it. We'll be needing empty tubs again before you're back, unless you hurry.'

Marion threw herself against her belt again, but the truck was full now and reluctant to move. She grunted as she thrust again and again, but it scarcely stirred. The leader drew his belt and lashed out at her bent buttocks and she cried out with the sudden pain, but her convulsive jerk got the heavy tub moving, and she kept it going as she crawled into the tunnel mouth again. First Charlotte, then I, followed, each smarting from a dozen blows of the strap which left our bottoms burning, but had at least given us sufficient impetus to move the trucks.

The return journey was a very different task to that which had brought us to the coal face, and its coarse crew. Now we had to throw our full weight against the belts just to keep them going. The chains tensioned and pulled up into our forks, the rough and dirty links digging painfully into the soft woman flesh between our legs, while our breasts swung uncomfortably beneath us as our bodies moved violently from side to side with the awkward all-fours progress. The sweat ran even more freely in the stiflingly hot passage, dripping from faces and chins, forming drops on the dependent teats, running into the tight creases of

202

our buttocks to sting and smart in their tender depths.

The coal dust not only smarted in our eyes, but got into all our orifices, causing havoc in the soft wet membranes of our female sheaths, the narrow creases at elbow and thigh, even causing our scalps to itch and burn. By the time the lights of the shaft bottom reappeared, we were exhausted and sore all over.

The overseer was not pleased to see us.

'You should have been here long ago,' he shouted, as we emerged into the comparative ease of the pit bottom. 'There's a quota to fill, and we'll never meet it if you're going to idle like this all day,' he told us, as he hooked us to fresh tubs for the return journey. 'If you're not back before the gang have filled the tubs you left, they'll have your hides. And what they don't take, I'll skin off you if you don't get back here to meet the cage,' he promised darkly, and sent us on our way with more vicious cracks of his solid leather belt.

We stumbled back down the track as fast as we could go, the pale moon-like buttocks of Charlotte in front of me rapidly disappearing into the darkness, only to slowly materialise as we reached the men's workplace again.

Once more they cursed us for our lateness in holding them up for lack of tubs. When they had unhooked the empties, they fastened our wrists to wedges driven into the coal face. It was not high enough to stand, but they made us kneel, then laid lengths of the timbers they used to prop the roof, across the backs of our calves, so that we could not move, and lashed our poor aching backs with their belts. They were tough hardy men, used to swinging picks in kneeling attitude, and their blows were as hard as any I endured. We all had tear streaks in the black grime on our faces when they finally released us, only to fasten us to full tubs and drive us out of the heading with more blows of their belts to our buttocks.

Evan cursed us for slowness when we returned to the shaft, but took no action. I think he could see from the state of our backs that the men had been there before him. We were hooked to new tubs, and crawled off painfully once more.

This time when we reached the workplace the men were having their 'snap'; drinking beer from bottles and eating out of kerchiefs on their knees. They offered us a share, which we accepted gratefully, but we had to pay for it, as all else down that pit. As we knelt again, for them to fasten our hooks to the full tubs for return to the shaft, other shafts came into play.

I felt a movement behind me and hands, not between my thighs to grasp the chain and, perhaps, give a rough caress to breast or vulva by the by, but on my buttock cheeks, prising them apart. I heard the noise of someone spitting into his hand, and something wet and sticky was applied to my cringing anus. Before I could protest, both hands were back in place but, more disturbingly, something blunt and hard nuzzled my anointed dimple. I resigned myself to the inevitable. After all, these were men in close proximity to naked women, and their juices must be boiling. We must do our duty and relieve them of the same, before it became injurious to their health.

I sighed for, despite our long experience of this duty, it

was always sore, and we had grime and grit enough in our tender places to ensure it might be especially so on this occasion. Nor was I wrong. The man was brutally direct, thrusting home in one movement, though he was mercifully swift, roaring his relief in no more than a minute, his flaccid member sliding out, leaving a sticky trail behind.

With belts and curses they drove us back into the darkness of the tunnel, and we threw ourselves against the belts, the soreness in our bottoms adding to our distress. We were sobbing with exhaustion and pain when we emerged into the light again, desperately dragging our protesting bodies along to try and avoid further punishment, this time at the hands of the overseer.

The rest of that first day is but a confused blur of pain and desperation in my mind. We toiled despairingly to keep up with the men's output, forcing our poor weak bodies to drag the heavy tubs up the incline to the shaft, lashed by the stinging belts of the miners and the overseer, until our bodies were blotched and inflamed all over under the overlying coat of grime that covered our sweat-soaked torsos. Every part of us was sore and aching, from our poor skinned knees to our abused bottoms and abraded vulvas, where the chains had rubbed them raw.

The heat in the workings was intense and humid, and long before the day was over we could smell ourselves, rank and sour.

When at last we were told we had pulled our last tubs for the day, we collapsed on the floor at the foot of the shaft, until the overseer's belt drove us to our knees again, to crawl into the cage and mount to the surface, the leather girths still tightly fastened round our waists.

In the shed at the top we helped each other remove them, wincing as the leather had to be drawn out of our flesh, so deeply had it been driven by the frantic pulling to move the recalcitrant trucks of coal. Each of us carried a red ring of fire about her waist, the edges raw.

There we remembered our clothes, which we had been made to discard at the foot of the shaft. But when we enquired of the overseer, he informed us that, as we would have no need of them while we worked in the haulage way, dragging coals, they had been collected and taken to the Hall for safekeeping. Meanwhile we might eat the food provided, and would sleep here, with the horses that worked the windlass, sharing their straw.

Later we learned the object was to protect and conceal us from the women strikers but, at the time, it seemed appropriate to us to share accommodation with the horses, since we were just as much draught animals as they. Before he left us, locking us in for the night, the overseer claimed Charlotte's bottom, needing to relieve his own pressures, but clearly heedful to his own advice to the miners that we were not to risk swollen bellies. Again, it came as a great relief to know that this would be so.

We looked to clean ourselves, but found only cold water from the pump. We were used to such ablutions, of course, they had been our daily lot for more than a year, but we could obtain no soap or other aid to removing the black grime on our skins. And though we were refreshed and our bodies no longer stank, as they had done in the heat of the mine, we could scarcely pass as clean.

We were woken before dawn the next day by the overseers shouts and smart kicks to our tender rumps, and given porridge, coarse bread and small beer for our breakfast. Adequate for the hard labour we were doomed to, but scarcely appetising.

Knowing what awaited us down the mine, we searched about for something to protect our knees, and came across some mouldy sacking that had held corn for the horses' feed, and tore this into strips which, together with a packing of straw, gave us some protection.

With this aid, and our bodies becoming used to the work, we made better progress day by day, satisfying our gang's need for tubs to take away their winnings from the coal face. For the next four weeks we toiled every day in the mine. We had no clothing, and our shelter remained the stable. The food was adequate, though plain, with enough at supper and breakfast to sustain us. But nothing provided for a midday meal in the middle of our twelve hour stint, and we had to join the colliers in their break if we wanted to eat, sharing their 'snap', but paying for it with the only currency we possessed, those assets that women always carry with them, the service of our bodies. Thankfully the men were in sufficient awe of the overseer to leave our virginities intact, our greatest fear, and to only use those rear orifices we had become used to making available for the purpose, for many months now, in our guardians' service.

It was a hellish time, but our bodies hardened and we came to terms with the life, bearing all for the concept of the dignity of labour, and our determination to show that women were not all idle creatures, loathe to be put to work in dirt and discomfort.

Eventually the women who had abandoned their allotted task saw the error of their ways, and we were told, at the end of our stint, that they would be returning to work the next day, and we were dismissed. To our request for clothing or transport we received only shrugs, and the information that there had been no instructions given as to our disposal. The overseer opined that, since Mr Brangwyn had been responsible for our recruitment, we should make our way to the Hall and look to him for help.

There being no other choice before us, we set off, naked and dirty as we were, to find our way thither.

No sooner had we left the shelter of the windlass house than there was a blood-chilling ululation from a crowd of ragged women waiting outside. They rushed upon us, screaming curses and foul language, calling us sluts and scabs, bosses bitches and the like and seized us, despite our protestations that we had merely been doing our duty as women, as we saw it, besides exploring the healthful experience of labour.

'Tar and feather!' went up the cry. 'Whip the whores until they bleed!'

Angry hands seized us and dragged us to the smithy, where a pot of tar stood ready always, to treat split hooves and such. The women threw us on our backs, ignoring our cries, dragged our legs open and slapped the tar brush, scalding hot, onto our poor tender vulvas, already raw from our long service in the mine, where the unfeeling chains had gnawed and worried at our female parts, hour after hour.

As we shrieked and writhed they pulled out our arms like starfish and thrust the still steaming brush under our hairy armpits, then turned us on our stomachs and filled our hair with the sticky black matter. Battered and burnt, I thought they had done their worst with us then, but some harpy screamed, 'Butter their arses,' and the hands pulled open our buttock cheeks, and thrust the hot brush between, drawing new screams from us as the hot tar touched the tender dimples in the cleft and left them sealed, as if for posting, but with black wax, not red.

Someone produced a feather pillow, ripping open the end, so that the fluffy contents fluttered down all over us, clinging to every part as they rolled us this way and that, until we were coated. Now they dragged us to our feet, and set our faces down the village street.

'The Hall is that way,' one shouted. 'Run to your master, you jezebels. Go and collect your blood money, scabs!'

We were only too anxious to obey but, before we could reach safety there was one last hazard. The women lined up along both sides of the narrow street, leaving just room for us to pass between. They were armed with long willow switches, lengths of rope knotted cruelly at the end, leather belts and slats of flat wood. We had to run the gauntlet of these viragos, their blows and cuts landing on every part. Instinctively we would put our hands to a particularly sore hurt and, whatever motion we made, it was bound to open up another part to cruel blows.

A vicious cut to my hinds had me reach behind to grab

the stinging cheeks, exposing my breast, which a screaming Amazon caught with a knotted rope. Eventually all three of us found the only way we could cope was to wrap our arms around our breasts to protect them, and run with heads bowed as best we could. Our backs and buttocks suffered terribly, and those who had armed themselves with ropes, as seemed to be a majority, for they gave the impression of having played this devilish game before, swung them up at us on our approach, and also as we passed, trying, and too often succeeding, to send the rope's end between our thighs and catch our poor abused vulvas.

By the time we reached the sanctuary of the lodge gates, we were all three in tears and some distress; bruised, battered and striped all over, and scarcely able to stand.

Instinctively we made our way to the kitchen entrance, not wishing to present ourselves at the front door, the entrance to which our station in life would normally entitle us. There we were met by a large female person in cap and apron who belaboured us with a broom, crying out to us to go away, she'd have no scarecrow harlots in her kitchen. Just as we were about to admit defeat and slink away, a male person appeared at her shoulder and quieted her.

'It's all right, Mrs Batser,' said he. 'Return to your duties. I will deal with this.'

The woman retreated, still muttering curses and waving her broom at us, as if it were a weapon. The butler turned his attention to our three tar-stained trembling forms.

'The master mentioned that three female persons might

be expected,' he said to the air above our heads. 'But that their condition might not be sanitary.'

He paused to sniff at our disgusting nakedness and bruised bodies, as if to convey that he had not expected us to be quite so insanitary.

'He gave instructions that you were to be sent to the stables for the grooms to clean up, and that you should stay there until your condition had improved sufficiently for you to be admitted to the house. You will find the stables where the drive continues behind the trees.'

We turned and limped away to follow the cruel gravel of the driveway, that felt to our bare feet as if walking on nails, and came upon the stable yard a little way from the house itself. Here we found a number of grooms and stable boys who greeted our appearance with hoots and cries of the most insulting and obscene nature, calling attention to our state.

'Never seen shit as black as this before,' ventured one.

'That's not shit,' his friend countered. 'They've been screwing the Devil himself. Old Nicks spunk is black and sticky.'

'I can believe it,' contributed a third. 'But how come it's in their hair? Buggered arses and fucked cunts are two-a-penny round these parts, but it's their mouths get used, not their scalps, usually.'

They had much amusement at our expense, but we cared not by then, for they fetched turpentine and linseed oil, and set to work to clean us up as well as might be done for a first effort. The turpentine stung our tender female parts, burning and causing us to writhe and squeal, but we submitted gratefully to their attentions.

They were not without their own motives for working on us so vigorously. For this service we had to pay in the usual currency and, since there were a dozen of them, and but three of us, the price was high, and harder still to bear, since our poor bums had been scorched by the hot tar. But it did at least ensure that that portion of our anatomies was made clean and proper for the purpose when, otherwise, it might have been left to cleanse itself naturally.

We stayed in the stables a week before our state was such that we could approach the Hall again, and seek admission. The men had been in no hurry to make us fit to depart, keeping our bodies or, at least, our nether openings, for their use as long as they dared. Not a night passed but we had to accept a line of four a-piece. I could not make up my mind which was the worst ordeal; the grooms, with hardened hands and lusty pricks, or the humiliation of having to bend and accept one of the stable boys, many years my junior. At least they were not so rough with us, and their adolescent pricks seemed not to distress our stretched anuses as much as the stallion sized cocks the men deployed, but to be taken there by a boy caused my soul to cringe.

At last the day came when we could persuade them to send a message to the house that we were fit to enter. The butler himself came out to inspect us and, although disparaging about the grime ingrained beneath our skins, and the traces of tar he still purported to detect in our pubic hairs, he grudgingly admitted we might just pass muster and that he would send out our clothes to us. We almost cried when a smirking maidservant arrived with a large basket containing the garments we had been made to discard at the shaft foot five weeks before. We had not worn a stitch of clothing since that time, exposed naked to man, woman and child, if one includes the stable lads, for all that time. Beasts too, if the horses in pit-head and stable are considered. We got our clothes, but for a price again, taking all the stable hands one last time, before we were permitted to cover ourselves at last.

Mr Brangwyn greeted us in an off-hand manner, as if we were guests who he couldn't refuse, but could spare little time for. He advised us that we would be found beds for that night and then, tomorrow early, we would take carriage back to our own home. No mention was made, then or later, of our work in the mine, the sufferings we had undergone, or indeed, the service we had rendered him by bringing to their knees the female strikers, who normally drew the tubs, by toiling in dust, dark and heat on ours.

And a surprise awaited us at the judge's home. Far from being neglected in our absence, the gentlemen had installed three girls to take care of those noxious effusions that, it seemed, so continuously troubled them. It was only natural, I suppose, that they should take measures to ensure their health, and we were very wicked to resent their presence, but they were brash and loud, and treated the gentlemen with much less than that deference to which they were entitled.

Moreover, we found that we were expected to wait on these rather ill-bred creatures with all the attention we paid our guardians, cleaning their rooms, doing their washing of the most intimate sort, and constantly at their beck and call, in addition to our normal duties and the stern disciplinary exercises to which we three sisters were subject.

Our evening disciplinary sessions were resumed, but the new girls not only were exempt, it seemed, from these inquisitions, and the subsequent fustigations, but were actually invited to comment on our behaviour, and most shaming of all, to use the rod on our backsides and even witness the use made of our private nether places subsequently.

I did remark on this to the judge, who informed me in stern tones that they, being of less fine clay than ourselves, were less vulnerable to female woes, and hence in less need of such disciplines. He also pointed out, quite legitimately, that my questioning of the arrangements made for the household smacked of impertinence, and I was awarded extra strokes at the evening chastisement, and put into the most cutting of crotch straps for three days without respite, emerging with my conscience cleared, and my ignorance enlightened.

Impregnation & Transportation

And now a new, and irrevocable change was thrust upon us. At dinner we were told to prepare ourselves with especial care for the evening's session in the study. Our persons were to be meticulously clean and neat, our female parts, especially, to be attended to and the hair about them trimmed of stray ends, our vaginas washed with soap and water, and to be sweet and scented. This was so far a departure from the usual austerity of our care that we could not help speculating among ourselves as to what it portended, but were still at a loss when we reported as required.

We found the gentlemen, as usual, accompanied by their new friends, drinking brandy and in rare good spirits. The judge called all to order and the session commenced.

It began conventionally enough, though the number of our faults, and the penalties awarded seemed much more than usual. I was made to mount the arms of the dread chair and take fifteen strokes from the bishop, and then stay on my painful perch while the young interloper, who was the bishop's favourite, lashed me with a further ten, keeping them all on my thighs, the most painful spot of all.

They did not however require us, as had been the custom, to remain with stretched forks on the chair, at the end of each of our fustigations, while they discharged their copious accumulations of harmful juices in our rectums. Instead, we were sent out into the corridor, then called in, one by one.

Marion went first, as was usual. From outside the heavy closed door we two who remained could hear but little; a murmur of voices, some loud laughter and inaudible remarks from the girls, and a sharp cry from Marion. The process of satisfying the judge's wants seemed to take rather longer than we were used to, or perhaps it was just the apprehension induced by being banished to the corridor.

Eventually Marion reappeared, her face covered in tears. She would not meet our eyes, or answer our urgent whispered queries, shaking her head and almost running towards her room.

Pale with apprehension, Charlotte went in to do her turn, and I waited, my belly now quaking, to listen to a repeat of the previous pattern, including some barracking, by its sound, followed by a shrill cry from Charlotte. There was a cheer from the girls, as if some deed of significance had been accomplished, then only vague noises for a minute or so. Some minutes later Charlotte appeared. Like Marion before her, she would not face me, but fled to her room as if forbidden to communicate.

I entered the study on legs of jelly. Previous experience had taught me that all change was usually for the worse, and likely to lead to pain, humiliation or both.

I made to strip my body, preparatory to mounting the chair, when the judge indicated he had something to say.

'Your other guardians and I have been giving careful

thought as to your best management and future course. We have come to a number of conclusions, which will be made known to you when the time is right. In respect of one of those decisions, that time is now.'

I trembled, wondering what this could mean; what dire experience had left my stoic sisters so distraught.

'It has been represented to us by your fellow females,' the judge indicated the three young women who had so lately joined the household, 'that your virgin state is a source of unhealthy pride to you, and a perpetual affront to them. Tonight, you will be relieved of that maidenhead, and your pride humbled, the affront wiped out.'

I must have paled for faintness overcame me, and I nearly swooned. So this was what my poor sisters had suffered, their maidenheads ripped so untimely from them. No wonder they had passed without speaking. Even if they had not been forbidden to say anything, shame would have kept them silent.

'Mount the chair, now,' the justice ordered. 'Since you have been the reverend bishop's special care, he will do you the honour of taking your flower.'

For a moment I stood open-mouthed, struck dumb with horror, trying to form words of protest and supplication, but it was in vain. In any case, my words would not have been heard, if uttered, for the horrid girls struck up a chant of 'Up! Up! Up!' and before their monstrous barrage, I capitulated and climbed onto the chair, skirts thrown up over my back, exposing my whip-streaked buttocks, my thighs widespread by the spacing of the arms, leaving my vulva open to the rear, the lips slightly stretched already by the pose.

While the hateful young women egged him on with cries of encouragement, the bishop unbuttoned himself, letting his manhood spring free. It was a mighty member, as I knew only too well from its frequent insertion into my tight anus, and I cringed at the thought of what it was about to do. I trembled as I felt it nuzzling between my nether lips, and probing for the sealed entrance to my vagina, while the girls called out lewd comments on his weapon.

'That's better than Salisbury spire,' one cried.

'Ring her bells for her then, bishop,' urged another.

And, 'Ram her, slam her, burst her pride,' from the third.

He began to push but my maidenhead was strong, and he could make no progress. It hurt abominably, and I might have been better off if it had been a lesser membrane, and given more easily.

The lustful harpies began another chant, 'Push! Push! Push!'

The bishop thrust with all his weight, and he was through, the mighty weapon sunk deep into my belly. My shriek of pain and shame was drowned in the cheer of vengeful glee that went up from the girls. They danced in triumph, calling, 'Who's a virgin now?' and, 'That's your pride pricked, slut.'

I clung to my perch in numb misery, scarcely concerned now that the bishop was battering me with his loins, his belly thwacking against my sore buttocks, his male member reaming my torn sheath. Only when his pace quickened and I felt the monstrous shaft swell within me, did the full horror strike me. He was about to discharge his seed into my unprotected belly and there was nothing I could do about it.

The lewd young women sensed his mounting passion also, and began to egg him on, chanting in time with his frenzied stroking, urging him to, 'Give it her. Pump her full, bishop. Stuff her to the gills.'

To the accompaniment of their cries, and strangled grunts from the bishop, I felt, for the first time, the frightening flush of semen against my womb.

That night I lay in my narrow bed, sore in buttock and vulva. Would that all the perilous fluid might leave, but I had no hopes that I might escape that way.

From then on this mode of intercourse became the norm, and we were taken in this fashion each evening, at the conclusion of our disciplining. The cruel interlopers were usually allowed to stay and watch our degradation and exposure to the risks of swollen bellies and ruin, while frequently they were allowed also, to suggest what punishments we should suffer, and even to inflict them.

After the first evening when we were deflowered, the gentlemen did not restrict themselves to their one usual sink into which to discharge their juices, but took each of us in turn, so that we received seed from all three, several times a week. It was almost inevitable that some of this abundant sowing should take root and, within two months, each of us began to show disturbing signs. Another month, and we could not dismiss them as fantasy brought on by fear. Each was now certain of a swollen belly, and milky teats. Our stays could not be made to meet, tug we never so desperately at their laces.

When we, as we must, confessed our condition to our guardians, they had the doctor strip and examine us, to confirm our findings, then had us stand while the judge told us how they intended to deal with us.

'Now that you have proved yourselves harlots by conceiving when not wed, we cannot allow you to remain in this house and sully its reputation by bringing bastards into it. Tomorrow I will convene a special court, where you will be condemned for harlotry, and sentenced to a whipping, and to transportation to the new penal colony in Australia.

But before then, you will hand over all that you possess to these young women, who will take care of our needs in the future. You may retain two plain gowns, two petticoats, two pairs of stocking and a pair of shoes each, together with a kerchief and hairbrush, some sewing necessaries, nothing more.'

And so it was done. At the special court the clerk read a disposition laid by the bishop, accusing us of harlotry, and the doctor gave evidence of our pregnancy. The judge gave a homily denouncing vice, and saying an example should be made. Besides, he added, the new colonies were short of females to populate the country and, with our proven fertility, we would serve well for the purpose.

At this point he turned again to the man of medicine.

'Is it your opinion, doctor,' he enquired, 'that these young women can sustain a good whipping, without danger to their bellies or themselves?'

'For certain, my lord,' our medical adviser replied.

'These are strong young women, in good health and well fed. Now that the bastard seed inside them has been attached to their bellies for over two months, there is little will jar it loose, as many a young woman has learnt to her cost, who has allowed her swain to swive her, admitting the flush of passionate seed into her fertility, then hoped by rigour and stress to shake it free.

'No, they'll take the whip, if that be your will, and no harm done. And a fine example to other young women not risk their bellies,' he added gratuitously.

Thus reassured, the judge pronounced our doom.

'I sentence you to be transported for life to the colony of Australia, and for a parting gift you shall be flogged in the marketplace before you go. Thirty strokes for each of you. God bless the King.'

And our fate was sealed.

That night we spent in the county jail, mocked by the wardresses who explained that we had not been taken straight from the court to be flogged, as was the usual custom, so that there might be time for the great ladies who lived about to come to see the sight, and revel in our sufferings for, they assured us, there was nothing these highborn dames loved better than to see one of their own class stripped and whipped, and better still if she were young and pretty. One such was a rare treat. Three was a sight they would be very wroth to have missed, and so our execution had been delayed sufficient that they might attend.

We slept ill that night on the thin straw that was all our bed, our thoughts filled with dismay and uncertainty as to what would befall us, buoyed up only by the thought that whatever the judge had ordered must be just and for our own good, for he had been acting in the name of the great British tradition of justice, rightly respected throughout the known world.

In the morning we were given a meagre breakfast of hard bread and a little small ale, and left to fend for ourselves until the hour appointed, noon, when the market would be crowded and the great ladies, and their escorts, might be assembled. There was little to do but fret about the coming ordeal, and sit nervously upon the pail in the corner, when our nerves tipped our bladders, or our bowels, into overflowing.

It came almost as a relief when, a little before noon, the chief wardress arrived, accompanied by a grim dark man, dressed in greasy leather, who one would not mistake for any other than the public executioner, whose duty it would be to flog our naked backs.

'This is Master Hackett, come to see what he has to work,' the wardress said by way of introduction. 'Get your stuff off, and let him feel your meat.'

We interpreted this as an instruction to bare our backs for his inspection, and duly shed our gowns. Since we wore no stays, we had but shifts, stockings and shoes left to us. By pulling down the straps of our shift we could bare our backs, though it left our swollen breasts exposed before. Master Hackett passed along the line, pinching up flesh between finger and thumb, as if assessing prize pigs at the show, to see if they would yield streaky bacon or fat.

'They'll do,' he said. 'Fine healthy specimens every one. None of your half starved hedge droppings here, but well padded flesh. They shall have their whipping, and more. No need to hold back on these fine ladies,' and he left us to the wardress's care, no doubt to make sure of his arrangements in the marketplace.

'Right my fine ladies,' the wardress mocked, taking her cue from the executioner, 'let us prepare. Women for public punishment go penitent and barefoot, so off with those shoes and stockings. It will help you feel humility on the way to the scaffold. You'll no doubt be feeling something quite different when you return. Master Hackett has a way of bringing blood to a woman's back, and tears to he eyes. He'll make you squeal, I warrant, before you tread this way again.'

With this cheerful intelligence she encouraged us to shed our footwear, and stand barefoot, clad only in our shifts. We had begun to raise the straps over our shoulders again, once Master Hackett had pronounced us prime meat for the slaughter, but the wardress checked us.

'Leave them be,' she ordered. 'You must show where you are to be whipped as you walk to your fate.'

We had hoped, at least, to have been able to cover our breasts with our arms, but even this was denied us for, as we came to leave the jail for our long walk through jeering crowds, we were each given a long bull's pizzle, the stretched and dried member of an ox, with which we were to be thrashed.

'A rod for your own backs, tradition says,' the wardress informed us. 'You must carry it in both hands, placed across your backs, where it will later fall. As to your breasts, full-bellied trollops have no room for pride, and must expose them to their teats to the common gaze.'

It was a hideous walk, full of shame and humiliation. We walked in line, but even then were made to leave such space that all could let their eyes rest on us freely, nothing concealed. Our shifts hung down over our gently swelling bellies, our figures maintained in some balance by our swollen breasts above, the distended globes forcing the turgid nipples into milky prominence.

All along our path people had gathered, many men calling rough obscenities, but even more women, whose lewd and cruel cries hurt more than the coarse male repartee, for the women seemed to hurl spite with their badinage.

We walked behind the beadle, who set a pace so deliberate and slow, he must have been paid by those who had no place by the scaffold, to hold us back as long as possible within range of their taunts and missiles for, as we slowly progressed, we had to endure a hail of clods of earth, dung from the gutters, rotten fruit and evil smelling eggs of ancient vintage. By the time we reached the scaffold we were mired from head to foot, our faces splashed, our hair and breasts dripping rotten egg, and stinking of it all.

We had expected to be taken one by one and whipped in turn, speculating gloomily during our incarceration whether it was better to be taken first, and have it over with, or be last, and have to endure the sight of our sisters being flogged before us. In the event we all suffered together.

The scaffold held three whipping posts, set on the points of a triangle and linked at their tops for strength and stability. Now we saw the reason we each carried our instrument of punishment, for the executioner had engaged two assistants, each as burly and uncompromising as himself, so that three lengths of bulls' leather might lash three white backs at once.

Each of us was led to her corner, and her wrists tied with leather thongs. Our bound wrists were then passed over a hook high on the post, until we were almost on our toes. Hands grabbed our ankles and drew them apart, wrapping them with more thongs and fastening them to the wooden platform on which the posts were erected to give the populace a fine view of our disgrace and suffering. With our feet spaced thus, we were up on our toes and could move but little, offering a steady target for the whip, unable to turn away from its bite when it began to gnaw our sides and under arms.

By now my position was so extreme, and my fear so overwhelming, I could spare little attention to my sisters' misfortunes, being wrapped up in my own, which were considerable. I was strung up tight against a rough wooden post which chafed my tender swollen naked breasts, while my bulging belly pressed against the same post lower down, though protected by my lowered shift. My arms were strained painfully above my head, as I stood on my toes. Numbly I awaited the flogging to which I had been condemned. Thirty strokes in public, from a bull's pizzle on my naked back.

All around me I could here the jeers of the women, especially the highborn dames who had paid to have the best points of vantage reserved for them. They chattered and called, made disparaging remarks about our breasts, and the swellings just discernible below our shifts where the seed was growing, and called us sluts and trollops, harlots and scarlet women. Their fervour was such I suspected some of them foamed at the mouth, and not only the mouth above their chins, either.

There was more harrowing delay, then a rattle of horse and wheels. I turned my head as best I could and there, seated in a carriage for which a space had been cleared not five yards from the scaffold, were the judge, the doctor and the bishop, and those horrid girls whose jealous importunities had led our guardians to deflower us and ensure our ruin. Now they crowed in triumph over our discomfiture, and our coming torment. God forgive me, for I wished that they could have been stripped and set in my place.

Now there was no more cause for delay. The sentence of the court was read, our thirty lashes confirmed, and the executioner was bidden to do his duty.

I closed my eyes and held my breath, and a line of fire exploded across my naked back. Another and another and another fell, tracing a hideous ladder of pain down my shoulders.

I was determined not to cry out before these leering ladies, and the crowing painted creatures in the judge's carriage, but it cost me much. I had of course been whipped many times before, but always on the buttocks or, very occasionally, on some excruciatingly painful intimate part of breast, belly or vulva. These whippings had been agonising, but something in their positioning made them become a part of one's most sensual being and, though the pain was still there, and not mitigated, nevertheless, this sensual connection made it not as devastating. To be whipped upon the back made no such connection. It was pure pain, of the most atrocious kind, and not a frisson of sensual response to compensate. I found myself beginning to despair after only ten strokes or so, and my strength slipping from me. The pizzle was long and supple and wrapped round my sides to bite into my armpit, or even caress the side of my full swelling breast. I could not turn away, and the executioner, who had chosen to lay on my stripes himself, leaving his assistants to cut my poor sisters' backs, seemed to sense my anguish at these bites, and let the tip out further so that it could reach my tenderest parts with every blow.

I think I would have screamed and pleaded for mercy at the next cut if I had not heard one of the horrid girls cry out, 'Hurrah, Master Hackett! Swing with a will! She'll sing soon, and her screams will be music to my ears. Lash her well, mister, and you shall taste my gratitude in my kisses. The blood on her back will be almost as sweet to my eyes as that on her thighs, the night I had them rend her maidenhead, the stuck-up little cow.'

I bit my lip and pressed my sore teats to the rough timber, inviting splinters, and they helped me to hold out and deprive the young bitch of her triumph. Sick and fainting, I took my strokes, not giving a sound.

My tally mounted, but I would not 'sing'. Though the last strokes nearly broke me I clung on, buoyed up by hatred of the young harlot in the carriage. She shrieked alternate abuse and promises at my whipper, calling him no man if he couldn't make a milksop wench like me cry out, offering him her tawdry body if he did. Little did she know that, if she'd kept her peace, she could have heard my screams a score of times before my tally of strokes was completed.

And so we travelled up to London, sore in body and mind, our backs a mass of welts, that vexed us sorely whether we tried to stand or sleep. We arrived at the dockside to find that the fleet was about to sail, and were driven up the gangplank with staves and sticks, told to hurry lest we miss the tide.

Now began a very troublesome time for the three of us. As fast as our backs healed, so our bellies swelled, until we became quite ungainly. With little time to prepare, and forbidden to take more than the judge had dictated, we had to rely on the rations issued on the ship, and the kindness of strangers. When the private stores were exhausted the women began to hunger, and made so bold as to ask the purser for better portions. He dismissed their requests contemptuously, and warned that any one asking again should suffer the rope's end on their buttocks.

'I'll warrant that'll make you dance,' he guffawed. 'Even the toughest tar will dance a jig when caught across his canvas seat with a tarry tawse.'

Matters got no better, and Marion persuaded us that we should be the ones to repeat the request.

'After all,' she pointed out, 'they would hardly whip women in our condition,' for, by then, our bellies proceeded us like sails.

With this thought to sustain us, we went to see the purser, and requested him politely to reconsider the women's rations for, as we pointed out, the authorities could hardly wish to have us delivered dead or dying, or so weakened by hunger that we would be of little use to populate the new settlements.

This seemed to touch him on the raw. Indeed we learnt later that he had a scale of doles laid down for him, and supplies to match, but hoped to keep a surplus and sell it advantageously in the new land. We were cursed for impudent sluts and in minutes found ourselves on deck, bent over a bollard, our mighty bellies pressed under us, our now generously fatted buttocks exposed, for our gowns were flung over our heads, muffling our cries and cutting us off from sight. While jesting seamen made coarse comments on our fleshy posteriors, they held us firmly in place, and the bosun's mate, summoned by the irate purser, laid into those same plump pillows with tarry rope knotted into hard knobs at one end. The pain of that heavy lash was as bad as anything I had suffered in the past – papa's penal cane note excluded. We shrieked and kicked under the whip, but the man did not stop until all our buttocks were welted solidly from top to bottom.

We crept back to our sisters in misery, sore, sobbing and defeated.

Still, it was not a useless gesture in the end. News of our brutal flogging came to the ears of the surgeon, for one was appointed to each ship by the authorities, anxious to reduce the number of souls lost on the voyage. He ordered us brought before him, to be inspected to see we had come to no harm in our expectant condition. We were a sorry trio, limping and groaning, but he looked us over, and pronounced us unharmed.

'For,' he said, 'the human female is a more resilient creature than many give credit for, able to endure much more punishment than that, even when big with child. Or half the children conceived would never come to term, since a man is entitled to chastise his wife, and in nine months will find himself with a dozen instances were provocation is so gross that a belt or rod is all that will cure it. Still, I'd like to see them better fed.'

This was our opportunity, and we took it.

'Sir,' I said, 'if you think we need more food, then consider the other poor wretches. They have given their all to help us in our condition, seeing each of us is eating for two. I beg you to inspect the generality of the women, and consider whether they are getting the rations they need, and to which they are entitled.'

There is much good in the man, for he listened to what we had to tell him, and came into the hold to see how the poor creatures fared. From then on the rations have improved remarkably, and the doctor is now often seen, observing their issue, to the scowls of the thieving purser. We are all in much better health and spirits, as we approach our destination, and for my sisters and I, our imminent deliveries. What will become of us then, I cannot conjecture, nor record, for I must close my narrative now.

This account of our history and salvation, that I have been writing to pass the long months of the voyage, has been made possible by the kindness of the chaplain who has furnished me with pen and paper, despite the captain's warnings of the dangers of encouraging women to attempt composition or thought, processes widely held to upset the balance of the unsteady female intellect, leading to hysteria, brainstorms and mental degeneration, and it is to him that I shall entrust it for safekeeping, in the hope that some day, other females may read of our experiences and derive suitable profit from them.

Epilogue

The foregoing account was found among what at first appeared to be mere mouldering rubbish in the attic of an old property in Sydney, when it was being pulled down to make room for modern development. The papers, tied with string and wrapped in oilcloth, were wedged into a crevice in the wall, which may explain how they had come to lie there for over a century and a half. It is believed that the building, one of the first to be erected in the colony, was occupied for many years by a man of religion, who had come out as chaplain on one of the early convict ships, and had stayed to minister to the new colonists. It would seem probable, therefore, that he is the generous gentleman referred to in the manuscript, who provided the writer with materials to set down her history.

The scholar, to whom it was passed for study, was able to link the three women to certain leading families of the city. At first glance one might be excused for thinking that these families might be proud to acknowledge ancestors whose children were fathered by a judge, a bishop or a doctor, but since no one was in a position to say which, and at least two of the sisters continued their mission of mitigating the sufferings of men by offering the use of their bodies for a small monetary consideration, one rising to become the Madam of a notorious brothel for sailors, the present editor has agreed to leave out any reference to surnames that might identify them. In this connection, he would like to thank the families concerned for the generous tokens of their esteem he subsequently received.

Exciting titles available from Chimera

* * *